Temporary Dad

Laura Marie Altom

HARLEQUIN®

TORONTO • NEW YORK • LONDON
AMSTERDAM • PARIS • SYDNEY • HAMBURG
STOCKHOLM • ATHENS • TOKYO • MILAN • MADRID
PRAGUE • WARSAW • BUDAPEST • AUCKLAND

ISBN 0-373-75078-1

TEMPORARY DAD

www.eHarlequin.com

Printed in U.S.A.

Annie gaped

What else could she do faced with the handsomest man she'd ever seen—hugging not one baby, not two babies, but three? Each red faced and screaming. Triplets?

"I'm your new neighbor, Annie Harnesberry. I don't mean to be nosy, but it sounded like you might need some help." She reached for the most miserable-looking baby and cradled the poor thing against her left shoulder.

The guy sort of laughed. "Yeah. My little sis left me with these guys over twenty-six hours ago. She was supposed to be back at two yesterday afternoon, but—" The babies launched a whole new set of screams.

"I'm Jed Hale. I'm a fireman. What do you do?" He awkwardly held out his hand for her to shake.

"I'm a preschool teacher now, but used to work with infants in a day care. I ran a pretty tight nursery." She winked. "No crying on my watch." Annie's triplet had calmed, so she brushed past her neighbor to place the child in a pink bunny-covered car seat. Then she took another of the screaming babies, and like magic, after a few jiggles he fell into a deep sleep.

"Wow," Jed said with a look of awe. "How'd you do that?"

Dear Reader,

My parents were both teachers when I was a kid, and every year, just as soon as school let out for the summer, we'd leave Michigan and head for the Colorado Rockies. My dad was an amateur gold miner, Mom was an avid reader and I liked both gold panning and reading, so usually a good time was had by all.

One not-so-happy part of our trips, though, was that my father claimed to be allergic to tourist traps. Back in the late seventies there seemed to be a lot of quirky Americana-type places. The World's Biggest Ball of Twine and The World's Deepest Well—can you believe it? Dad actually stopped at that one! Anyway, this book is a realization of all my childhood tourist dreams—especially when Jed and Annie get to stay in a real cabin. To save money, we always stayed in a tent. Brrr!

Back when I was a kid, Colorado was gloriously empty. We'd spend whole weeks seeing hardly anyone. As a kid, I grumbled quite a bit about these family camping trips, but now I look back on them as a truly magical time. Thanks, Mom and Dad!

Would you like to share your vacation adventures with me? Please write me at BaliPalm@aol.com or P.O. Box 2074, Tulsa, OK 74101. Like your vacations tropical? Hit my beach at lauramariealtom.com!

I hope all of you enjoy Jed and Annie's story.

Laura Marie Altom

This book is dedicated to the wonderful game
of Scrabble, and to all the lovely folks
with whom I've had the privilege to play.

John Chew, webmaster extraordinaire
for the National Scrabble Association—
thanks so much for your generosity in sharing the
particulars of the National Scrabble Championship.
Any errors in official protocol are mine.

Chapter One

Waaaaaaaaaaaa! Waa huh waaaaaaaaahh!

Sitting in a cozy rattan chair on the patio of her new condo, Annie Harnesberry looked up from the August issue of *Budget Decorating* and frowned.

Waaaaaaa!

Granted, she wasn't a mother herself, but she'd been a preschool teacher for the past seven years, so that did lend her a certain credibility where children were concerned. Not to mention the fact that she'd spent the past two years falling for Conner and his five cuties. Considering how badly he'd hurt her, the man must have a PhD in breaking hearts.

Baby Sarah had only been nine months old when Conner brought his second-youngest, three-year-old Clara, to the school where Annie used to teach.

Their initial attraction had been undeniable— Annie's affinity for Clara and Baby Sarah, that is.

The two blue-eyed blondes were heart-stealers.

Kind of like their father, who'd gradually made

Annie believe he'd loved *her* and not her knack for taking care of his children.

The man had emotionally devastated her when, instead of offering her a ring on Valentine's Day, he'd offered her a position as his live-in nanny—right before showing off the diamond solitaire he was giving the next female on his night's agenda.

Jade.

His future bride.

Trouble was, Jade didn't much care for the patter of little feet—hence Conner's sudden need for a nanny. But beyond that, he explained that the exotic brunette was one hot ticket. *Us all living together'll be like a big, happy family, don'tcha think?*

Waaaaa ha waaaah!

Annie sighed.

Whoever was in charge of that poor, pitiful wailer in the condo across the breezeway from hers ought to do *something* to calm the infant. Never had she heard so much commotion. Was the poor thing sick?

She plucked a dead leaf from the pot of red impatiens gracing the center of her patio table, then returned to her article on glazing. She'd love to try this new technique in the guest bath that was tucked under the stairs.

Maybe in burgundy?

Or gold?

Something rich and decadent—like the decorating equivalent of a spoonful of hot fudge.

The house she'd grown up in had been painted top

to bottom, inside and out, in vibrant jewel tones. She'd lived with her grandparents, since her mom and dad were engineers who traveled abroad so often that once she'd become school-age, it had been impractical for her to go with them. Her second place of residence—never could she call it a *home*—had been painted mashed-potato beige. This was the house she'd shared with her ex-husband, Troy, a man so abusive he made Conner look like a saint. Lodging number three, the apartment she'd run to after leaving her ex, had been a step up from mashed potatoes, seeing how it'd been painted creamed-corn yellow.

This condo was her fourth abode, and this time, she was determined to get not only the décor right, but her life. As much as she loved spending five days a week around primary colors and Sesame Street wallpaper, in her free time, she craved more grown-up surroundings.

Waaaaa waaaa waaaaa!

Waa huh waaaa!

Waaaaaaaaaa!

Annie slapped the magazine back onto her knees.

Something about the sound of that baby's crying wasn't right.

Was there more than one?

Definitely two.

Maybe even three.

But she'd moved in a couple of weeks earlier and hadn't heard a peep or seen signs of any infant in the complex—let alone three. That was partially why she'd chosen this unit over the one beside the river, which had much better views of the town of Pecan, Oklahoma's renowned pecan groves.

The problem with the other place, the one with the view, was that it catered to families, and after saying tearful goodbyes to Baby Sarah and Clara and their two older brothers and sister, not to mention their father, the last thing Annie wanted in a new home was children.

Conner had packed up his kids, along with his gorgeous new wife and Scandinavian nanny, moving them all to Atlanta. The children were just as confused by the sudden appearance of Jade in their father's life as Annie had been. She sent them birthday cards and letters, but it wasn't the same. She missed them. Which was why she'd left her hometown of Bartlesville for Pecan. Because she'd resigned herself to mothering only the kids at work.

Conner was her second rotten experience with a man. And with trying to be part of a big, boisterous family. She sure didn't want any daily reminders of her latest relationship disaster.

No more haunting memories of running errands with the kids at Wal-Mart or QuikTrip or the grocery store. No more lurching heart every time she saw a car that reminded her of Conner's silver Beemer on Bartlesville's main drag.

She needed a fresh start in the kind of charming small town that Conner wouldn't lower himself to step foot in.

Annie looked at her magazine.

Glazing.

All she needed to feel better about her whole situation was time and a can or two of paint.

Waa huh waaaaaaa!

Annie frowned again.

No good parent would just leave an infant crying like this. What was going on? Could the baby's mom or dad be hurt?

Wrinkling her nose, nibbling the tip of her pinkie finger, Annie put her magazine on the table and peered over the wrought-iron rail encircling her patio.

A cool breeze ruffled her short, blond curls, carrying with it the homey scent of fresh bread baking at the town's largest factory, a mile or so away. She had yet to taste Finnegan's Pecan Wheatberry bread, but it was supposedly to die for.

Normally at this time of year in Oklahoma, she'd be inside cozied up to a blasting central AC vent. Due to last night's rain, the day wasn't typical August fare, but tinged with an enticing fall preview.

Waaaaaaaa!

Annie popped the latch on her patio gate, creeping across grass not quite green or brown, but a weary shade somewhere in between.

The birdbath left behind by the condo's last owner had gone dry. She'd have to remember to fill it the next time she dowsed her impatiens and marigolds.

Waaaaaa!

She crept farther across the shared lawn, stepping

onto the weathered brick breezeway she shared with the as-yet-unseen owner of the unit across from hers.

The condo complex's clubhouse manager—Veronica, a bubbly redhead with a penchant for eighties rock and yogurt—said a bachelor fireman lived there.

Judging by the dead azalea bushes on either side of his front door, Annie hoped the guy was better at watering burning buildings than poor, thirsty plants.

Waaa huhhh waaa!

She took another nibble on her pinkie.

Looked at the fireman's door, then her own.

Whatever was going on in there probably wasn't any of her business.

Her friends said she spent too much time worrying about other folks' problems and not enough on her own. But really, besides her broken heart, what problems did she have?

Okay, sure, she got lonely now that she lived an hour south of her grandmother. And her parents' current gig in a remote province of China meant she rarely got to talk to them. But other than that, she had it pretty good, and—

Waaaaaaa!

Call her a busybody, but enough was enough.

She couldn't bear standing around listening to a helpless baby cry—maybe even more than one helpless baby.

Her first knock on the bachelor fireman's door was gentle. Ladylike. That of a concerned neighbor.

When it didn't work, she gave the door a few hard thuds.

She was just about to investigate the patio when the door flew open. "Patti? Where the—oh. Sorry. Thought you were my sister."

Annie gaped.

What else could she do faced with the handsomest man she'd ever seen—hugging not one baby, not two babies, but three? Each red faced and screaming. Triplets?

On teacher autopilot, she reached for the most miserable-looking one, automatically cradling the poor, trembling thing against her left shoulder.

"Hi," she said, lightly jiggling the baby while at the same time smoothing her fingers down the back of her head—her judging by the pink terry-cloth pjs. "I'm your new neighbor, Annie Harnesberry. I don't mean to be nosy, but it sounded like you might need help."

The guy sort-of laughed, showing lots of white teeth. "Yeah. My, um, little sis left me with these guys over twenty-six hours ago. She was supposed to be back at two yesterday afternoon, but—"

Annie's triplet had calmed, so she brushed past her neighbor to place the child gingerly in a pink bunny-covered car seat. Then she took another of his screaming babies for herself.

"Don't mean to be pushy," she said, "and please, go on with your story about your sister, but occupational hazard—I just can't stand hearing a child cry."

"Me, too," he said, wincing when the baby he held launched a whole new set of screams. "I'm a fireman.

Jed Hale. What do you do?" He awkwardly held out his hand for her to shake.

"I'm a preschool teacher now, but used to work with infants in a day care. I ran a pretty tight nursery." She winked. "No crying allowed on my watch."

"Admirable." He grinned, and his boyish-yet-all-man charm warmed Annie to her toes.

She soon calmed the second baby, then put him—judging by his blue terry-cloth pjs—alongside his sister in a blue giraffe-upholstered carrier.

She took the remaining infant in her arms, and, like magic, after a few jiggles he fell into a deep sleep.

"Wow," the boy's uncle said with a look of awe. "How'd you do that?"

Annie shrugged, easing the last snoozing triplet into his seat. "Practice. My major was premed with a minor in child development. Seems like I spent half my college career in the campus nursery studying infants. They're fascinating."

He leaned against the open door. "Sounds pretty bookish for a preschool teacher. I didn't even know you had to go to college for that—I mean, not that you *shouldn't* have to, but—"

"I know what you mean. I always wanted to be a child psychiatrist. Not sure why. Just one of those things." She didn't have a clue why she was standing here in this stranger's home, spilling her guts about stuff she hadn't thought of in years. Reddening, she said, "Sorry. Didn't mean to ramble—or barge in. Now that you've got everything under control, I'll just mosey off to my magazine." She backed out of his condo and hooked her thumb toward her patio. Whew.

The man's eyes were gorgeous. Brown shot with the same flecks of gold she'd like on her bathroom walls. Opulent and rich and definitely all grown-up. As yummy as that spoonful of hot fudge swirled with caramel! The decorating version of course...

Although she wasn't in the market for a man herself, should she try fixing him up with one of the other teachers at her school?

"Don't leave," Jed said, hating the needy whine in his tone. He'd always prided himself on never needing anyone, but this woman he didn't just *need,* he had to have. He had no idea what magic she'd used to zonk out his niece and nephews. However, if his sister didn't arrive to claim her offspring in the next thirty seconds, it'd be a pretty safe bet he'd need Annie's special brand of baby tranquilizer all over again. "Really, stay," he said, urging her inside. "I've been meaning to bring over a frozen pizza or something. You know, do the whole Welcome Wagon neighbor thing. But we've had some guys out sick and on vacation, so I've been pulling double shifts." He glanced at his watch. "In fact, I'm due back in a few hours, but my sis should be here way before then."

Now who was the one rambling?

Jed could've kicked himself for going on and on. Not only did he have a desperate need for this woman, but now that he'd been standing next to her for a good fifteen minutes, he was starting to admire more than her babysitting skills.

She was cute.

Hot in a G-rated sort of way.

Loopy blond curls kissed her shoulders and neck. A curve-hugging white T-shirt gave tantalizing peeks at cleavage and a great, all-over tan. And seeing how she was now up to a PG-13, how about those great legs in the jean shorts?

Damn.

Not too long, not too short. Just right for—

Waaaaaaaaa!

Triple damn.

He sure loved Patti's little critters, but they were in serious need of a few lessons on how *not* to screw up Uncle Jed's chances with his hot new neighbor.

"He's probably hungry," she said, marching over to the carrier and picking up his squalling nephew. "Got any bottles?"

Her lips. Man. When she talked they did this funny little curvy thing at the corners. Made him want to hear her talk about something other than babies. Where she'd moved from and where she one day wanted to go. Why she'd wanted to be a child psychiatrist but ended up teaching preschool.

"Jed?" Annie grinned. "You okay? If you'd just point the way to the bottles, I'll go ahead and feed this guy while you take a breather."

"I'm good," he said with a shake of his head. "The bottles are in here."

He led her to the kitchen. A tight, beige-walled cell of a room he usually avoided by eating at the station or feasting on takeout in front of the TV.

He took a bottle from the fridge, then turned to the woman behind him. "Want me to nuke it?"

She grimaced, kissing his nephew on top of his head. "It's probably best to put the bottle in a bowl of hot water, otherwise it gets too hot."

"Oh."

She headed toward the sink.

Speaking of hot...

Nudging on the faucet, she asked, "Got any big bowls?"

Jed retrieved the only bowl he owned—a promotional Budweiser Super Bowl VIII popcorn dish he'd won playing sports trivia down at his friend's bar. "This work?"

She eyed it for a second, then said, "Um, sure."

OVER AN HOUR LATER, Annie had fed and diapered the infant trio. Jed had confirmed her earlier assumption of their being triplets. The five-month-old girl was named Pia, and the boys, Richard and Ronnie. Jed explained earlier that morning, he'd lost the ribbon bracelets his sister kept on the boys to help tell them apart, so now he wasn't sure who was who.

"Man," he said, arching back his head with a yawn.

"I don't know how I'll ever repay you. When Patti finally shows up, she's going to catch heat the likes of which she hasn't felt since I caught her smoking in church."

"Bit of a wild child, was she?" Annie asked, as she fastened the last snap on Pia's pink jammies. She found a tiny pink Velcro bow stuck to the terry cloth, pulled it off, and attached it to the baby girl's thin tufts of hair.

He laughed. "That's an understatement. The happiest day of my life was when she said her *I Dos* to Howie. Finally, I thought, she's someone else's responsibility."

"You been looking after her for a while?"

"Yeah. Our folks died my freshman year of college. Patti was okay as a kid, but once she hit her teens, she was nothing but trouble. She started pulling all this rebellion crap. Smoking. Drinking. Exclusively dating guys whose gene pools were only half-full. Most times, I knew she must have still been upset about Mom and Dad. But then there were other times I swear she did every bit of it just to piss me—" He winced. "Sorry."

"That's okay," Annie said, hugging the sleeping beauty to her chest.

"So lately," he said, "she's been kind of depressed. Howie—her husband, my savior—got laid off from his job here in Pecan, so he took a new one that has him traveling out east a lot. The company won't pay for the whole family to relocate, so until he can find something closer to home, this is what he's doing to pay the bills. Patti hasn't handled it all that well. Before this happened with Howie, she'd been a bit shaky on the whole motherhood thing—not that she hasn't done a great job. It's just that she gets pretty frazzled."

"Who wouldn't?" Annie said, starting to share Jed's concern for his sister, this precious infant's mother. She stroked Pia's downy-soft hair and breathed in her innocence and lotion.

"Anyway, that's why I offered to watch these guys for her. I figured she could use a little break, but her being gone overnight…" He shook his head. "I never agreed to that. I've checked her house, called her neighbors and friends. Mrs. Clancy on the end of her block saw her tear out of her driveway yesterday about twelve-thirty in my truck. Since I can only fit one baby seat in my truck, she probably thought it best to leave me with the Baby Mobile. No one's seen her since." He raked his fingers through his hair.

The muted sound of a running vacuum came from next door.

"When she was younger," he said, "she ran away a few times. I'm scared she's choosing that way out again. But it could be something else. Something bad…"

The vacuum went off.

Annie leaned forward, her stomach queasy. "Have you called the police or tried getting in touch with Howie?"

He shrugged, then pushed himself up from the sofa

and began to pace. "I've got a couple friends down at the police station, so I've been calling them like every hour. They've entered my plates and Patti's vitals into the national missing persons base. Anyway, the cavalry's been called, but they keep telling me the same thing. Wait. She'll come home. There's been no sign of trouble. Odds are, with Patti's history of running, the stress of the babies probably got to be too much for her and she just took off."

"And her husband? Did you ever get hold of him?"

"Nope. His cell keeps forwarding to voice messaging—same as his office phone. Apparently, not a single real live person answers the phone at that high-tech fortress where he works. I'd go to see him, but he's out in Virginia somewhere."

"Sorry," Annie said. "Wish there was something I could do."

"You've already helped," he said. He shot a glance at his nephews. "Sometimes when these guys—and girl—start on a crying jag, I get panicky. Maybe my sister felt the same and split."

Annie's eyes widened. "She just left her babies?"

"I don't want to think that of her, but what other explanation is there? I mean, if there was an emergency or something, wouldn't she have called?"

"I'd think so, but what if she can't?"

"Oh, come on." He stopped pacing and thumped the heel of his hand against a pasta-colored wall. A snow-capped mountain landscape rattled in its chrome frame.

"In this day and age, I'll bet you can't give me one good reason why a person *couldn't* call."

Annie wanted to blurt dozens of comforting reasons, but how could she when Jed was right?

Chapter Two

Patricia Hale-Norwood glared at the ICU nurse manning the desk phone. "*Please.* I'll call collect. I just need to let my brother know where I am. I left in a hurry, and he'd taken my triplets to the Tulsa Zoo, and so I couldn't—"

"I'm sorry," said the steely-eyed, middle-aged dragon disguised as a nurse. "Hospital policy. This phone is for emergency use only."

"This *is* an emergency." Heart pounding at double the rate of the beeping monitor in Room 110, Patricia clenched her fists. From the call that'd interrupted her bubble bath telling her Howie had been in an accident and was barely alive, to the hasty trek down the front porch stairs that had badly sprained her right ankle, then the endless flight and rental car drive that led her to this North Carolina hospital where her husband now drifted in and out of consciousness, this whole trip had been a horror show that just kept getting worse.

The nurse sighed. "I'm sorry, but unless you're in

need of a blood transfusion or have an organ you'd like to donate, I can't let you use this phone. There are pay phones and courtesy phones located throughout the hospital for your convenience."

"Look." Patricia slapped her palms on the counter. "I don't know if you're aware of this or not, but over in that fancy new wing y'all are building, some yo-yo sliced the phone cables with a backhoe. So now there isn't a single phone on this whole freakin' square mile that works— except for yours—which, I've heard through the hospital grapevine, has its own separate emergency line."

"*Please,* Mrs. Norwood, lower your voice. We have critically ill patients here."

"You're damned right!" Patricia said shrilly. "My husband happens to be one of them. He's hanging on by a thread, and you're acting like he's here for a bikini wax. Now, we've been through this already. My cell batteries are dead. My charger is back home two thousand miles away. My ankle's swollen to the size of a football, making it kind of excruciating for me to get around. *Please* let me use this phone."

The nurse cast Patricia a sticky-sweet smile. "Perhaps a family member of one of our other patients has a cell they'd allow you to use in the special cellular phone area on the sixth floor?"

JED SLAMMED his cordless phone on the kitchen counter.

What was the matter with those guys down at the police station? They were supposed to be his friends.

Hell, Jed had been the one who'd thrown Ferris his police academy graduation party. And now the guy was claiming there wasn't a thing more he could do to find Patti?

He glanced at his niece and nephews, thankfully all still sleeping.

What would he have done without the help of his new neighbor? What was he going to do when all three babies woke at the same time, demanding bottles and burping and diaper changing?

Jed had earned many medals for bravery as a fireman. Yet those snoozing pink and blue bundles made him feel like a coward.

The phone rang and he lunged for it before the next ring. "Patti?"

"She's still not back?" said Craig, one of his firehouse buddies.

"Nope."

"What're you gonna do? We need you down here, man. There's a brushfire on a field by the country club, and we just got back from a house-fire call over on Hinton."

"Anyone hurt?"

"Nah, but their kitchen's toast."

"Bummer." Jed had been on hundreds of scenes like this. Witnessed lots of *why me's* and crying. Crying. Occupational hazard.

Annie said the same about her job. How she hated hearing babies cry. Jed hated hearing *anyone* cry. It was great that he saved lives, but the emotional toll taken by fires was every bit as horrible as the physical destruction.

Fire didn't just ruin lives and houses, it also stole memories.

Snapshots of Florida vacations.

Golf and baseball trophies.

Those goofy little clay ashtrays kids make in kindergarten.

Little brothers.

He sighed into the phone.

"Jed, the chief's real sorry about your sister, but we need you down here. Want me to call Marcie and ask her to watch the triplets for you?"

Marcie was Craig's wife.

And yeah, she could come sit with the babies, but that would be about the extent of it. Those two didn't even own a dog or a guppy. What did she know about taking care of three newborns?

But Annie...

She'd know what to do.

The way she'd calmed his niece and nephews earlier that day—it'd been a bonafied miracle.

"Jed? Want me to tell Chief when you'll be in?"

"I'll be there as soon as I can."

"Will do," Craig said. "Catch you later."

Jed pressed the phone's off button.

He hated asking for help.

After his parents had died, he'd looked after not only

himself but his sister, who'd been ten. He was nineteen then, and he'd done a good job. Their folks' life insurance hadn't lasted long, and when it'd run dry, he'd finished college at the University of Tulsa, taking night classes. Worked his tail off during the day making sure Patti had everything a kid could want.

The bank took the house they'd lived in with their parents since after the fire, but he'd found them an apartment over the old town theater. The whole building had long since been condemned, but back then, they'd played dollar movies there on Thursday, Friday and Saturday nights.

When Patti was still a sweet kid, he'd taken her to most of the shows. No R-rated ones, though—his mom wouldn't have approved.

He'd come close a few times to having to sell the cabin in Colorado that'd been in their family for generations. Money had been crazy tight, but somehow, he'd made things work. That cabin was the only tangible reminder of their parents. A part of Jed felt that he owed it not just to Patti, but to his own future children to keep it in the family. No matter what the personal cost.

He'd single-handedly raised his sister. He'd gone over her homework, helped her study for tests. Gone looking for her when he suspected she was hanging with the wrong crowd. Grounded her when, sure enough, he'd caught her guzzling beer down by the river.

He'd even been there to rub her back when she'd

thrown up those beers a few hours later in the apartment's rust-stained toilet.

He'd covered college applications and tuition. Book and dorm costs.

Through all of that, he'd never asked for any help himself.

Never wanted it.

But now…

Somehow this was different.

Helping Patti study for a test? That he could do. Dragging her home from a party? Paying her student loans? He could do that, too. But figure out how to care for three babies while launching a full-fledged investigation into Patti's whereabouts?

He groaned.

If this afternoon was any indication of the fun still ahead, his sister's latest stunt just might do him in.

Jed sighed, resting his elbows on the kitchen counter. "Patti, where are you?"

Ten minutes later, propping his front door open with a bag of rock salt he'd found in the coat closet, Jed did the unthinkable—knocked on Annie Harnesberry's door to ask for help.

"JED. HI." Annie ran her fingers through the mess on her head. Ever since leaving her neighbor's, she'd been hard at work on her guest bath, scraping the shoddily applied popcorn ceiling, making way for something grander. A nice, restful Scrabble game would've been

more fun, but difficult with only one player. Hmm....
Someday she'd have to see if her new neighbor liked to
play.

"Looks like you've been busy." He brushed a large
chunk of ceiling from her hair.

Not sure whether to feel flustered or flattered by his
unexpected touch, Annie fidgeted with the brass doorknob. "One of the reasons I chose this condo was its
great bone structure. Redecorating is a hobby of mine."

"Great. Maybe you could tackle my place when
you're finished. We could talk tile over pizza."

"Maybe." Though his tone had been teasing, something about the warmth in Jed's eyes led Annie to wonder if he might be at least a little serious about wanting
to see her again. Was that why he was there?

To ask her out?

Wow. She'd just made this big move designed to
steer her clear of all men, yet here she was, faced with
another one. Even worse, the old optimist in her, the one
who so badly wanted to find that elusive pot of gold at
the end of the dating rainbow, had almost said yes. After
all, the guy *was* movie-star gorgeous.

Not that appearance mattered in the scheme of things.
Look what had happened during her first go-around with
a good-looking guy. Her ex-husband, Troy, had been
gorgeous. He'd also turned out to be her worst nightmare.

"Do you like Scrabble?" she blurted, not sure why.
Both Troy and Conner had hated the game that was her
family's passion.

"Love it," Jed said. "Sometime, when my life calms down, we'll have to play. I warn you, though, I'm pretty good." He winked.

Her stomach fell three stories.

No. No matter how handsome her new neighbor happened to be, she wasn't—*couldn't be*—interested. Yes, she'd date again because she couldn't bear the thought of ending up alone. But not yet. Her head and heart just weren't ready.

"Well—" He shuffled his feet.

From across the breezeway, Annie noticed his propped-open front door, and beyond that, the corner of a blue bassinet. "Your sister's still not back?"

"No. I'm really starting to freak out."

"I don't blame you," she said, squelching the urge to comfort him with a hug. At work, she hugged parents and students and co-workers, but in this situation, a hug might imply a certain affection she shouldn't want to share.

"The reason I'm here," he said, shooting her a beautiful smile that did the funniest things to her breathing, "is that all hell's breaking loose down at the station and they need me ASAP. So, anyway, I was wondering if you could hang out at my place for the next twenty-four hours? That's the length of my shift—but I'm sure Patti'll be back way before then."

"You mean you want me to babysit?" Handsome Jed Hale wasn't here to ask her on a date but to care for his sister's triplets.

She should've been relieved, so why did Annie's heart sink? Why didn't men see her for *her*, but only for her knack with kids?

Worse yet, why did she care?

Hadn't she just established the fact that she had no current interest in any man?

"Yeah. Babysit. Oh—and of course I'll pay. What's the going rate?"

Bam. Annie's ego took another nosedive.

Now the guy was even bringing money into it?

Why couldn't he just offer to take her out for a nice *friendly* steak dinner once his sister finally showed up?

"Annie? What do you say? Can you help me out?"

Noooo, she wanted to scream.

Hanging out with kids was her day job.

At night, she did grown-up things like scraping ceilings and glazing walls and sipping wine and playing Scrabble.

And if she was honest...

Dreaming of what her life might've been like had she met a guy who didn't hit or take advantage of her ability to move an infant from screaming to sleeping in twenty seconds.

What were the odds of a woman being so cursed in love?

"I know it's short notice and stuff," he said, those intriguing brown-gold eyes of his eloquently pleading his case. "But I really could use your help."

"Okay," Annie finally said, hating herself for being

so easily drawn in by Jed's puppy-dog sadness. She had to remind herself she wasn't doing this for him, but for the babies.

If she'd learned anything during her years with Conner, it was that guys with ready-made families were only after one thing. And it had way more to do with heating up formula than anything that went on in the bedroom. "What time do you want me over?"

He winced. "Would now be too soon?"

ANNIE LOOKED UP from her seat at the end of Jed's black leather sofa and came uncomfortably close to keeling over in an old-fashioned swoon.

Wow.

He stood at the base of the stairs, dressed in plain uniform navy cotton pants and a bicep-hugging navy T-shirt with a yellow Pecan Fire Department logo on the chest pocket. His choppy, short dark hair was damp from the shower.

He'd shaved, and the scent of his citrus aftershave drifted the short distance to where she sat. The mere sight of him, let alone his smell, implied clean, simple, soul-deep goodness. He was a fireman, charged with keeping helpless grandmas and grandpas and babies and kittens safe from smoke and flames.

It probably would've sounded crazy had she tried to explain her sudden reaction to the man. But in that moment, she knew he would never hurt her—at least not physically, the way Troy had.

"I can't tell you how much I appreciate you doing this for me," he said.

"Sure. It's no big deal."

"Yes, it is." He walked the rest of the way down the stairs. "You hardly know me, yet you're giving up your time to help me out. In my book, that makes you good people."

His words returned the warm tingle to her belly. She stood, not sure what to do with her flighty hands or dry mouth. "I already told you," she said. "It's no biggie."

He looked at her for a long moment, then peered down at his black uniform shoes. "To me, it's a very big deal. Don't discount the value of what you do."

The urge to hug him came back. In those opulent eyes of his she'd caught a glimpse of sadness. Fear for his sister? Or something more?

Before she had time to ponder the question, *he* was hugging *her,* wrapping her in his all-masculine scent and strength.

And his touch wasn't awkward or inappropriate, but comforting and warm. And then, just as unexpectedly as the sensations had come, they were gone, and Jed was waving and walking out the door. Thanking her again. Smiling again. Alerting Annie to the undeniable fact that she was very much in trouble with a man and his adorable children—all over again.

HOURS LATER, Annie woke to a ringing phone.

It took a few minutes of fumbling in the dark to realize she'd fallen asleep on Jed's sofa instead of her own. Another few minutes to actually find the phone—or not.

Somewhere, an answering machine clicked on.

Hey—congratulations! You've reached Jed. Leave a message and I'll call you back.

Annie grinned.

During the time they'd spent together, Jed hadn't shown any signs of having a sense of humor. The notion that he did made him that much more appealing.

"Jed," a woman's voice said. *"Good grief, it's after midnight out there. Where are you? Are my babies okay?"*

Patti.

Hoping she'd find a phone attached to the machine recording the woman's voice, Annie hustled up the stairs.

"You wouldn't believe the trouble I've had finding a phone. Anyway, I'm all right, but—"

By the time Annie got to the top of the stairs, dashed across the short hall and into a master bedroom that was the mirror image of hers, it sounded as if the woman had been cut off.

Annie found the phone on a nightstand beside a badly rumpled king-size bed.

She answered but was too late. The dial tone buzzed in her ear.

She turned on a lamp and checked the phone for caller ID, but the cordless model didn't have an ID window. She tried *69, but got an error message.

Great.

If the woman on the phone had been Patti, it seemed that she either didn't want to be found or was having technical difficulties.

Annie sat on the edge of the bed.

From talking to Jed, she got the impression that he thought his sister had suffered some kind of emotional breakdown, then taken off on a joyride. But the woman on the phone sounded weary—not at all like she was off having fun. Her voice was full of concern—quite the opposite of a woman who'd abandoned three newborns with her bachelor brother. A brother who obviously didn't know the first thing about caring for infants.

Waaaaaaa huh waaaaaaa!

Maybe it was time to quit playing detective and start playing temporary mom.

She smoothed the down-filled pillow on the bed and breathed in the room's heady male scent.

Oh, boy.

Annie had the feeling she'd entered a definite danger zone.

Bedrooms were highly personal places.

They told a lot about people.

But since she was wasn't interested in dating just yet, Annie didn't want to know how sumptuous Jed's navy-blue sheets felt against her skin. Or how they smelled of fabric softener and just a touch of his aftershave that had already made her heart race.

She especially didn't want to see the really great

framed print over his bed. Gauguin's *And the Gold of Their Bodies*.

She'd always loved that painting.

Interesting that Jed did, too.

The full-figured island women evoked paradise and pleasure.

Waaa huh!

On her way out of the room, Annie trailed her fingertips along the cool, dust-free surface of an ornate antique dresser.

She loved antiques.

The stories behind them.

Where had this piece come from? Was it a family heirloom? Or something Jed picked up at auction? Did he like auctions? Annie did. Maybe they could go together some time? Share a Frito-Lay chili pie during—

Waaaaaaaaahh!

Casting one last curious look around the room, Annie hustled downstairs.

She'd scooped Pia out of her carrier and was feeling her diaper for thickness when the phone rang.

If it was Patti, she wasn't missing her.

Running up the steps, Annie cursed herself for not bringing the cordless phone downstairs.

"Hello?" she said, out of breath. By the glow of the lamp she'd forgotten to turn off, she stared into the blue eyes of a grinning, wide-awake baby.

"Hey, Annie. Good—you found the phone." There went that curious flip-flopping in her stomach. Could it be because Jed sounded as hot over the phone as he did in person? No. And to prove it, she changed her focus to plucking Pia's pink Velcro bow off her pajama sleeve where it was once again stuck to return it to her hair.

"Were you hiding it?" she asked.

"What?"

"The phone."

"Nah, I keep forgetting to move it. Lightning fried the one downstairs."

"Did you serve it with ketchup or tartar sauce?"

He groaned. "That stank."

"Sorry. Couldn't resist."

"You're forgiven. So? Everything going okay?"

"Sure. Pia's up, but the boys are still sleeping. Oh— and your sister called."

"You didn't get to talk to her?"

"It took me forever to find the phone, and by the time I did, she'd been cut off."

A long sigh came over the line.

Annie asked, "Want me to play the message for you?"

"Sure."

She pressed the red button beside a blinking light, then held the phone to the speaker. When the woman's voice abruptly ended, she said, "Well? That tell you anything?"

"Yep. Tells me to call off the cops and move on to Plan B."

"What's that?"

"Going to get her."

"But you don't know where she is."

"Oh, yes, I do."

Annie shifted the cooing baby to her other arm. "Care to let me in on the secret?"

Chapter Three

In the specially designated cell phone waiting area, Patti held an ancient-model cell phone over her head, waving it back and forth in the hope of finding a signal. The man she'd borrowed it from, Clive Bentwiggins of Omaha, was visiting his mother. Clive was at least ninety-eight and on oxygen. The hissing from his portable tank sounded like wind shushing through the Grand Canyon.

"Get one yet?" Clive asked, cradling a cup of black coffee.

Edging toward the Coke machine, holding up her phone arm, Patricia shook her head. "I had one over by that fake ficus, but I—oh, here. Right here." *Yes.* Between the Coke machine and a corral of IV poles, the light indicating a signal glowed an intense green.

"Dial fast," Clive said. "Don't want you getting cut off again."

She cast her phone benefactor a smile and dialed Jed's number. It rang three times before the answering machine picked up. After the beep, she said, "Jed? Jed, honey, are you there? Jed!" She heard static on the line. *Crap.* She inched closer to the IV poles, but the green light disappeared.

Wheeling his hissing tank behind him, Clive walked toward her. "Losing it again?"

Patti nodded, tears welling in her eyes.

Where could they be?

Something had to be wrong. It was too late for Jed not to answer his phone.

He didn't have a woman over, did he?

She should've known better than to leave her babies with him.

The green light came back on, but all she could hear was the hissing from Clive's tank.

Covering the phone's mouthpiece, she said, "Would you mind scooting your tank just a little bit that way? I'm having a hard time—" Too late. The signal was gone.

Patricia sighed.

Clive patted her back. "I raised six kids and twenty-three grandbabies. Trust me, your flock is fine. It's that busted-up husband of yours you need to worry about."

"HELLO?" Annie said, hands on her hips. "Care to finally let me in on your big secret?"

Jed had been home from his twenty-four-hour shift for five minutes. In those five minutes, he'd replayed Patti's latest message ten times. Now he *definitely* knew where his sister had gone.

He shot into action, barreling into the kitchen. He'd take everything Patti left with him. There were only a few cans of formula and three or four diapers, but that should at least get him over the Colorado state line. In Denver, he'd grab whatever else he needed.

"Jed?" Annie's sweet voice jolted him from his to-do list.

Arms laden with his few requisite supplies, Jed looked up on his way back to the living room. "Yeah?"

"What are you doing?"

"Packing."

Annie's eyes narrowed as she kissed the top of Pia's head. "Please tell me you're not planning to load up these sweet, sleepy babies and trek them wherever you think your sister may be."

"Hey," he said from the living room, dumping the baby grub into the diaper bag, "I can see why you might think I'm crazy to go traipsing blindly across the country. But for your information, I happen to know exactly where Patti is."

"Oh, you do?" She followed him into the living room and gently set Pia on a fuzzy pink blanket on the floor. "Mind telling me how you worked it out, Sherlock?"

"Love to, Watson." He grinned. "You like those old movies, too?"

Frowning, she said, "I prefer the books."

"*La-di-da*."

She stuck out her tongue. "Just get to the part where you unravel the mystery."

"Simple deduction." He snatched the diaper wipes from the coffee table. "Remember all that hissing and shushing on the answering machine message?"

"Yeah…" she said, arms crossed, eyebrows raised. "Can't wait to hear where this leads."

"She's at our family cabin just outside Fairplay, Colorado."

"You've got to be kidding. Patti hardly said two words on that message, and from that you've deduced she's holed up in some cabin?"

Snatching a few teething toys—plastic key rings and a clear plastic thingamajig with fish floating around inside—Jed said, "You know babies, right? Well, I know my sister. Ever since having the triplets, she's had a rough time of it."

"Duh."

He shot his smart-mouthed neighbor a look.

She shot him one back.

Try as he might to stay on topic, Jed couldn't help thinking that he liked this feisty side of her. As soon as he got things settled, he just might tackle a whole new case—figuring out how to take Annie's PG-13 rating to a wicked-fun R!

He shook his head to clear it of the sweet sin threatening to muck up the next task on his road-trip agenda.

"Well?" she asked. "You're zero-and-one. Gonna go for zero-and-two?"

Jed glanced up as he stuffed a blue blanket into his now-bulging duffel bag. "Anyone ever tell you that for having such a fine package, you sure have a sassy mouth?"

Annie's face reddened and she looked away.

Hmm… Apparently he'd just pulled off his first TKO. "For your information, Little Miss Sassy Pants, all that hissing on the answering machine wasn't *hissing,* but wind. Wind whistling through the pines and firs outside our family cabin to be specific. Cell-phone service is touchy up there, which explains why she constantly gets cut off."

As much as Annie hated to admit it, Jed's warped logic made perfect sense.

"Patti loves the place. When our folks were alive, we spent every summer up there for as long as I can remember. After they died, Patti and I went there as often as we could. Here in town, she was all about keeping up appearances. I guess she felt she had to put on this cool act. But up at the cabin, she was herself. A sweet kid who allowed herself to have fun."

"But Jed—" Annie crossed the small space cluttered with stuffed animals to touch his arm "—she's not a kid anymore. She's a grown woman with a family of her own. If your assumptions are true—that she ran off to figure out her life—maybe what she *doesn't* need is her big brother charging in for a needless rescue. Maybe she needs time to get her head on straight. I mean, that's essentially why I moved here. I miss my grandmother something fierce, but it was time for me to grow up. To face a few issues on my own. I'm betting Patti feels the same."

Annie looked down to see that she was still touching him, and she marveled not only at his physical strength—tightly corded and radiating heat beneath her fingers—but at his sheer mental will.

"Look," he said, "I realize that I probably seem a little psycho right about now."

"A little," Annie said with a smile.

He didn't return her smile.

Instead, he dropped the baby bag and sat hard on the bottom step. He cupped his forehead. "There are some things about me. My past. Patti's. There's no time to rehash it all now. You just need to know that I have to get up there. See for myself that she's all right."

"Okay." Her tone softer, Annie nudged him aside to sit next to him.

Big mistake.

The entire right half of her body hummed. All the way from her shoulder to her thigh to her bare ankle that almost touched Jed's bare calf. The ankle felt a twitchy, electrical buzz of attraction that she—and her ankle— had never come close to feeling before.

This was wrong.

Here she was, trying to comfort her distraught neighbor and all she could think of was what it might feel like to graze her smooth-shaven legs against the coarse hairs on his.

Wrong, wrong, wrong.

"Um—" She swallowed hard. "Where was I?"

"How should I know?"

"Right. That's it." Before plopping down beside him, she'd been about to explain how he could find out his sister was safe without driving hundreds of miles. "There's a very simple way you can not only reassure yourself that Patti's okay, but skip a lo-o-ong road trip with three babies. All you need to do is—"

"I know—call. But the cabin doesn't have a phone, and I already tried her cell. Big surprise, it's not working. Which leaves me calling my friend Ditch, who's the local sheriff."

"Ditch?" She raised her eyebrows.

"It's a long story. Anyway, I tried calling Ditch both at home and at work, and got nothing but answering machines. I left messages for him to call me back ASAP. The town has a hardware store, gas station and a grocery, so I called those, too. Nobody's seen her, but that doesn't mean she's not there. I have to talk to her and see for myself that she's okay."

"I'll tell you who's *not* gonna be okay after being cooped up with three screaming babies all the way to Colorado."

Jed shook his head. "Babies supposedly like cars, don't they? I mean, I took 'em to the zoo yesterday— or was that the day before?" He rubbed his forehead. "See how messed up Patti's got me? I don't even know what day it is."

"All the more reason for you to go upstairs and take a nap. You're in no condition to make that drive. You've been up for days. Now, if you could fly or take a train or if someone else could help you, then—"

"That's it!" he said, turning around on the steps to face her.

Annie crinkled her nose. "What?"

"Someone to help. And I know just the person."

Though Jed looked straight at her, Annie glanced over his shoulder at the pasta-colored wall. A nice sage-green would be a vast improvement.

She gasped when he put his fingers beneath her chin, dragging her gaze right back to him. "You know who I'm talking about, don't you?"

"Um…" She licked her lips. Maybe that wall could be painted celadon. Or pumpkin. Any color that took her mind off Jed's arresting eyes. "If that special someone is me," she said, "I have a *very* full schedule. I start my new job a week from Monday. So, this week, I have tons of painting to do, ceiling scraping and—"

"I'll pay you," he interrupted. "Name your price. As long as I have that amount in savings, it's yours."

She stared down at her lap where she clutched her knees with a white-knuckled grip. "This isn't about money, Jed."

It was about this crazy yearning she had at the thought of sitting beside him in the intimate confines of a car for the next few days. It was about falling for him—from his laugh to his smile to the fact that he honestly believed four diapers and a few cans of formula were going to get him and three babies all the way to Colorado.

He hadn't even packed a can opener!

He needed her, and what scared her even more was that she might very well need him. But she *couldn't* need him, because just as soon as this crazy road trip was over, his need for a babysitter would vanish, and her need for companionship would be that much stronger.

Her head and heart that much more messed up.

"Annie?" he said softly. "Please?"

She used the wall for leverage to push herself up from the stairs. She had to get away from Jed, from his citrusy smell and his strength and, worse yet, his vulnerability.

Friends told her she worried way too much about other folks' problems and not enough about her own.

Well, this was one time she needed to listen to their advice. Her friends were right. Jed and his adorable crew were trouble with a capital *T*.

She stood in front of the door staring at the doorknob. "I have to go." *I can't allow myself to fall for you.*

She was still too raw from Conner. And she hadn't even begun to sort out the mess Troy had made of her soul. She was weary from missing Grams and from being all alone in this town—and practically the whole world.

Jed stood too, and then he was behind Annie, resting his strong hands on her shoulders.

"Ever since our folks died," he said quietly, "Patti's been my responsibility. She was a good kid—the best.

She was also the *worst* teen. I've been through hell with her. The night she gave up her virginity to the first greasy-haired punk who asked, it was me she came home to. I was the one who held her while she cried. Just like when I found her underneath a highway overpass in a seedy part of downtown Tulsa. She'd run away because she'd gotten mad at me for making her wash the dishes. She was shivering, and I wrapped her in a quilt our mother had made for her fifth birthday. It matched the yellow-and-white daisies on Patti's bedroom walls. When our house burned down, Mom had wrapped the quilt around Patti as we fled."

His hands still on her shoulders, Jed turned Annie to face him, which only upped the stakes of the battle raging inside her. Standing behind her, he was dangerous enough. When he stood in front of her, staring at her, she found that just looking at him was emotional suicide.

She'd already been through so much.

She couldn't open herself up to more pain.

Her move to Pecan was about healing. Making a fresh start. It was about—

Jed took her hands and gave them a gentle squeeze, flooding her with the kind of simple, wondrous, unconditional companionship she hadn't felt in years. Except that it wasn't unconditional; it came with strings. Strings that would vanish the instant they reunited Patti with her babies.

"I—I have to go," Annie said, turning for the door, putting her hand on the cold brass knob.

"Howie's her husband," Jed said. "He should be with her right now. But I can't find him, Annie. Until I do, I'm all she has. I have to help her. She's all I've got."

Annie swallowed hard.

How had he known?

Of all the words in the English language, those were the ones that spoke the loudest to her heart. It was exactly the way she felt about her grandmother.

"Annie, I'll be the first to admit I've got a mile-long streak of pride running through me. I hate asking for help. Even worse, I hate needing help. But in this case—"

"I'll do it."

"You will?"

Lips pressed tight, fighting silly tears of trepidation, maybe even excitement, Annie nodded.

Jed pulled her into a hug, and the sensation was warm and comforting, like slipping into a hot bath. This sure wouldn't make it any easier to fight her feelings for this man.

Releasing her, he clapped his hands, then rubbed them together. "Great! Let me tackle a few quick errands. I'll beg, borrow or steal time off from work and we'll get this show on the road. I'm assuming you'll need to call your folks? Or your grandmother? Or—" he crossed his fingers for a negative on this one "—your boyfriend?"

Annie shook her head. "The only family I have is my grandmother, and there's no need to worry her with a short trip like this."

"You sure?"

She nodded. Why even broach the subject with Grams? The older, wiser woman would think she was nuts—which she probably was.

"All right then. If you wouldn't mind hanging out here just a little while longer, we'll be good to go. Oh— before I forget…" He took a cell phone from the coffee table and plugged it into a nearby charger. "Is your cell battery fully charged?"

"I don't have a cell phone."

"How come?"

"I'd rather spend the fifty dollars a month on decorating supplies."

He smiled. "I knew I liked you. Finally, a woman who actually prefers an activity to talking."

"I didn't say I don't like to talk." She winked. "I just don't want my conversations to cost more per year than a custom-upholstered sofa and love seat."

Chapter Four

It was nine the next morning before they finally pulled onto Highway 75 leading out of Pecan and into Tulsa where they'd catch Highway 412. Annie had talked Jed into taking a nap that'd thankfully turned into a decent night's rest. Meanwhile, she'd run to the store for a more realistic stock of formula, diapers and diaper wipes, and also managed to grab a little shut-eye for herself while the babies were sleeping.

During her brief time away from Jed's formidable appeal—not to mention that of his niece and nephews—she'd given herself a nice, long pep talk.

Jed was *just* her neighbor.

And yeah, he was gorgeous, but that didn't necessarily mean she was falling for him. She was a big girl. So why was she so confused? Why did she feel that by agreeing to what should be nothing more than a brief road trip, she was essentially giving away her heart?

Could it be because that heart of yours hums whenever the guy's within three feet?

Annie cracked open the map. "Want me to find some shortcuts?"

Both hands on his sister's minivan wheel, Jed shook his head. "I'm an interstate kind of guy. I see no reason to tempt fate."

"Oh." She slipped off her sandals and propped her bare feet on the dash. Admiring her fresh pedicure, she said, "Don't you just love this shade of pink? The silver sparkles look like there's a party on my toes." She glanced his way and caught him rolling his eyes.

Eyebrows raised, he asked, "Do you have to do that?"

"Do what?"

"Get your dirty feet all over the clean dash. I just dusted it this morning."

"My feet aren't dirty—or dusty." She twisted in the seat to display her soles for inspection. "See?"

Barely ten minutes into the trip and the woman nearly had him crashing the car! Jed cleared his throat, thankful for that *keep your eyes on the road* rule, otherwise, he'd be sorely tempted to take the bottoms of those squeaky-clean feet and—

Nope.

Not going there.

This was a family trip.

G-rated all the way.

For an instant, he squeezed his eyes shut and took a deep breath. Did she have any idea that when she'd raised her feet for inspection, she'd also raised the frayed bottoms of her jean shorts? The sweet curve of her behind had him thinking anything but sweet thoughts!

He tightened his grip on the wheel.

"Tell me about Ditch," the constant temptation sitting beside him said.

He was grateful for the change of topic. "What do you want to know?" he asked.

"For starters—" she hiked her feet back onto the dash "—please tell me that isn't his real name."

"Nah. We used to take walks down our dirt road, and every time we heard the tiniest little noise, he'd hit the ditch, sure it was a bear."

She crinkled her nose.

Was it wrong of him that such a simple thing gave him such a peculiar thrill?

"If it *had* been a bear," she said, "why did he think getting in the ditch was going to keep it away?"

Jed laughed. "Good question, which is why the other kids and I gave him such a hard time."

"Poor guy. Did he ever—"

Waaaaahuh!

"What's the matter?" Annie asked one of the boys. "Already needing a snack?" She took a pre-warmed bottle from an insulated bag, tested the formula's temperature on her wrist, then offered it to Jed's nephew, who promptly batted it away. "I'll take that to mean he's not hungry," she said.

Waaaaaaahuh!
Waaaaaaa!

Great. Now Pia had joined in.

"Good Lord," Jed said. "We haven't even made it to Tulsa and already they're crying? I thought babies liked car rides?"

"Most do," she said above the racket, "but I guess these guys are the exception. Well, except for Richard. He's sound asleep."

"How do you know that's Rich?"

"Technically, I don't. But he has slightly thicker eyebrows than his brother, so that helps me tell them apart."

Sure. Why hadn't he thought of that? Jed sighed.

"What? You think I'm making that up?"

"When we make our first stop in Kansas, I'll take a look."

"*Kansas?* I hate to burst your bubble there, but judging by the howling, we're going to have to stop way before we even reach the Kansas Turnpike."

"The hell we will." And to prove it, Jed stepped on the gas.

FIVE MILES DOWN the road at a run-down picnic stop where hot, dry wind rustled scattered litter on the ground, Jed scowled.

All three babies wailed.

"This place doesn't look very clean," he said.

"It's not like we're going to roll your niece and nephews across the pavement."

"Yeah, well, all the same," he said over Pia's especially heartfelt cry. "Maybe we should just—"

Annie unfastened her seat belt and hopped out of the van.

Jed looked at the sun-bleached concrete parking area and the shabby picnic tables and shook his head.

An empty two-liter pop bottle rolled like tumbleweed until it stopped against the carved wooden sign urging folks to *Put Litter In Its Place.*

Annie slid open the van's side door. "Listen to you all," she crooned to the bawling trio. "My goodness. The way you're carrying on you'd think some TV exec canceled *Sesame Street.*"

She unbuckled Pia and scooped her from her seat. After patting the rump of her pink shorts, Annie said, "What's up, sweetie? Your diaper's dry." While talking to Pia, she rubbed Ronnie's belly. "Seeing how they tossed their bottles, I'm guessing they're not hungry, which leaves general crankiness as the cause of all this angst. Come on," she said, awkwardly taking Richard from his seat, too. "You grab Ronnie and we'll take them for a quick walk."

"A walk?" Jed had stepped out of the van and was standing behind Annie. "We were supposed to be halfway to Colorado by now. This is going to completely blow the schedule."

"What schedule?" Two babies and a fat diaper bag in her arms, she backed out of the van. "Think you could help me down from here? I don't want to trip."

Suddenly, Jed didn't just have lost time to worry about, but Annie's soft curves landing against his chest.

He caught her around her waist, guiding her safely to the ground, getting himself in trouble with the trace of her floral perfume.

"No, no." He shook off his momentary rush of awareness to remember his argument. "Why are you leaving the van? It'll just take that much longer to load back up."

Already halfway across the lot, aiming for the nearest picnic table, she called over her shoulder, "Could you please grab Ronnie? Now that we're stopped, I'd like to do an official diaper check."

Muttering under his breath, Jed did Annie's bidding, cringing when he reached the table only to find her spreading the babies' good changing pad across the graffiti-and-filth-covered concrete slab.

"What's the matter?" she asked mid-change on Richard, her right hand efficiently holding the gurgling baby's feet while she wiped him with her left.

Pia sprawled on a blanket Annie had spread beneath a frazzled red bud. The little faker was grinning up a storm while gumming the baby-friendly rubber salamander he'd bought for her at the zoo.

"What's the matter?" he echoed, hands on his hips. "These kids are bamboozling us."

Annie shot him an entirely too chipper smile. "Jed, they're just over three months old. There's no way they could systematically set out to mess with your schedule."

"Yeah, well, what else explains *this?*" He held out Ronnie, who was also alternately giggling and cooing.

Annie looked up only to hastily look back down.

She returned her attention to sealing the tapes on Richard's diaper, then resnapping the legs of his short-sleeved cotton jumper.

Why did she have the feeling that a whole lot more than the beating sun and dry Oklahoma wind were making her cheeks hot?

Like the sight of entirely-too-handsome-for-his-own-good Jed wearing Ray-Ban sunglasses, camo-green cargo shorts and a white T-shirt, while holding tiny little Ronnie so tenderly in his arms.

Once he learned to loosen up, Jed would make a great father.

Obviously not to any children of hers—just some lucky woman he had yet to meet.

"Okay," she said with forced cheer, hoisting Richard into her arms. "Pia's bone-dry, so let me check Ronnie's diaper and we should be good to go."

"So she faked all her tears, too?" He sighed.

Annie gave him a dirty look, suddenly annoyed when she ended up a little too close to Jed in order to give Ronnie's diaper the pat test. "He's dry, too," she said, turning quickly, planning to grab Pia and her blanket, along with the diaper bag.

"Wait," Jed said, his fingertips brushing her forearm.

Even with the breeze, the August air was stiflingly hot, yet somehow each individual imprint of his fingers on her skin felt hotter. She looked at Jed. "Yeah?"

"Thanks."

The breeze blew strands of hair into her eyes, and since her arms were full with Richard, Jed used his free hand to sweep away the stray curls. "What for?"

"What do you think?" He stared at his baby, then hers. "Much as I hate to admit it, you were right. There's no way I could've made this trip on my own. So in case I get too wrapped up later on—thanks."

His grumpy attitude about their first pit stop?

Forgiven.

"You're welcome," she said, afraid to look at him for fear she'd be that much more attracted. "Wanna put Ronnie in his seat while I grab the princess?"

"I'll get her and the gear," he said. "You be the brains and beauty behind this operation. I'll be the brawn."

Beauty, huh?

Settling Richard in his carrier, then climbing back into her own seat to feign interest in the map, Annie realized that trying not to fall for Jed would be about as easy as keeping three babies content for the next eight hundred miles.

"Y'ALL KEEP a good eye on those cuties!" The burly tow-truck driver waved, then veered into the heavy stream of back-to-school traffic clogging Wal-Mart's lot.

One arm around Richard, the other around Pia, Jed said, "When I get my hands on that no go brother-in-law of mine, I'll—"

"Calm down," Annie said. "It's only a flat." She took

Pia from Jed and placed her in front of her brothers in the three-seat stroller.

Jed snorted. "A flat that could've been fixed on the side of the road in under ten minutes. But *no-o-o-o*. Howie's the only man in the world who lets his wife and children drive around without a spare."

Hand to her forehead, Annie shielded her eyes from the baking sun. "You never know. Maybe they used the spare and haven't had a chance to replace it."

"Don't," Jed said, steering Annie toward the automotive section of the store.

"Don't what?"

"Try making this easy for my sister. Even if that no good brother-in-law was too lazy to replace the tire, Patti knows better. How many times have I told her always to be prepared?"

Annie laughed. "Like you were prepared to call a tow truck by forgetting to grab your cell from the charger? We were lucky that Triple A guy stopped for us on his way to work."

"I told you not to remind me about my cell phone."

"Sorry. Just thought poor Howie needed defending. Besides which, I think you're too hard on yourself. Things happen. You can't always be in control."

Wanna bet?

Yeah, forgetting his phone was a major screwup—right up there with not checking for a spare himself. But no more. From here on out, this trip would be run with military precision.

They'd reached the podium-on-wheels the tire guy used to write up their ticket. Jed held his jaw tight through the entire ordering process, during which the tire guy explained how the popularity of the back-to-school tire special meant his department was running about two hours behind. But there was a waiting area for their convenience.

"Sir?" the tire guy said. "Your keys?"

Jed fished in his pockets for the gaudy pink rabbit's foot key chain his sister had given him. It wasn't there.

Realizing what he'd done, he groaned.

"Sir? Your keys?"

Annie giggled. "You left them in the van, didn't you, Mr. Always Prepared?"

"AREN'T THEY SWEET?" Annie said, eyeing the three sleeping angels while slurping the last bit of cherry heaven from the bottom of her Icee cup.

Jed, who'd just finished checking his messages—or lack thereof—from a payphone, growled.

"Oh, come on," she said. "Would you get over it? Everyone makes mistakes. I lock myself out of my car all the time, which is why I now keep a spare key in a little magnetic box under the front wheel well."

"I've got one, too," he said, "only it's under the truck bed. Fat lot of good it's doing me there when I'm driving my sister's stupid van."

Fingertips aching to reach out and touch him, Annie toyed with a potato chip instead. "Are you more upset with your sister or yourself?"

"What do you mean?"

"I mean, why are you so angry? Are you still fired up about the missing spare tire? Or is your miserable mood more about the keys?"

Ever the pillar of responsibility, even when it came to his choice in drinks, he took a swig of bottled water. "Just drop it, okay?"

"Now what are you ticked off about?"

Jed pretended to be captivated by a pink, blue and yellow cotton candy display. "Do you think yellow is banana flavor?"

"Yes. And I also think you're avoiding my question."

"How do you know it's banana?"

She sighed. "Because it's my favorite and I buy it all the time. Back to the important stuff. Are you avoiding my question?"

"Absolutely. Now would you mind dropping it?"

"*Excu-u-u-use* me," she said, pushing herself up from the table to put her cup and remaining chips in the trash. Was it just him, or had her hands been shaking when she'd dumped the stuff? "I'll be in the clothing section until the car gets done, okay? While you were off grabbing all that auto emergency stuff, I changed everyone's diaper and filled fresh bottles, so you shouldn't have any trouble watching the babies by yourself."

Right before she left, she snatched a tiny pink Velcro bow from Pia's PJ sleeve and put it in her purse. "It's evidently a choking hazard," she said. "Kind of like looking at you."

"Dude, you got schooled," said a baggy-clothed punk passing Jed's booth.

Huh? Ignoring him, Jed just sat there, watching Annie walk away. Dammit. Why the hell hadn't he said something? He should've tried to explain.

His sister's selfish disappearing act already had him wound tight, but this latest fiasco?

He was now a man on the edge.

Elbows on the sticky table, cradling his face in his hands, he closed his eyes and took a few deep breaths.

Calm down, man.

Keep the past in the past.

Just like his little brother Ronnie's death had been out of his control, so was everything happening right now. That was the bad news. The good news was that all he had to do was hang tight until they got to the cabin, then everything would be fine.

Yeah, right.

Who was he kidding?

Here he'd been snatching peeks at Annie's long legs all afternoon, dreaming of the moment they turned the munchkins over to his sister so he could ask his hot neighbor out on a proper date. But if he kept up this gloom-and-doom routine, she'd refuse to even climb back into the van.

Jed looked down at his niece and nephews—all three of them still snoozing.

After another deep breath, he let the calm of knowing that at least the three of them were safe and content spread through him.

Patti was safe, too.

In the cabin. Probably trashing it with gossip magazines and pop cans and Oreo crumbs.

By the time he got there, the place would no doubt be mouse-infested, but that was all right.

As for his future nightlife…

He snatched a bag of banana-flavored cotton candy from the display.

Time for some major sucking up.

"I'M SORRY, ma'am, but I'm afraid you'll have to—"

"No!" Patti cried, fighting to get past the nurse keeping her from Howie's room. "He's my husband. It's my right to know what's going on." A few minutes earlier, she'd been holding Howie's hand, telling him how much the babies had grown in just the week he'd been gone. The room had been peaceful. Silent except for the soft whir of air-conditioning and the sound of her voice. And then that awful beeping had started, and—the rest was too horrible to think about. "I *have* to see him," Patti begged, hot tears stinging her eyes. *"Please."*

"Mrs. Norwood, let the doctors do their work. They'll tell you everything just as soon as your husband is stable."

Patti wanted to fight—really, she did, but at the moment, she was just too tired.

The kind nurse put her arm about Patti's shoulders and guided her into the dimly-lit waiting area that had become Patti's new home.

What she wouldn't give to be back at her old home.

Holding all three babies on her lap while Howie changed the TV channel fifty billion times with the remote.

"Are you going to be all right?" the nurse asked, settling Patti into a recliner.

Numb with fear, she nodded.

"Can I get you anything? Coffee? A blanket and pillow?"

My husband.

Please tell me he's going to be okay.

Chapter Five

Twenty minutes later, pride swallowed, Jed found Annie in the women's clothing department, holding up two metallic jogging suits against herself that, in this heat, would bake her like a foil-wrapped potato.

"In case you haven't noticed, it's a hundred and fifteen degrees outside."

"A hundred and *one,* and I don't remember asking for your opinion," Annie said. "Besides, if I wait to buy these until the time of year I'll really need them, the stores will be carrying bathing suits."

"True." Jed laughed. "And it can get chilly in the mountains—not that we'll be there that long, but—"

"Who said I'm going anywhere with you?"

"I got you this," he said, retrieving the cotton candy peace offering from the stroller's back pocket.

Refusing to meet his eyes, Annie shook her head, then turned back to the jackets. "You hurt me. I barely even know you, yet you really hurt me."

"I'm sorry," he said, slipping in between her and

the clothes. "I'll be the first to admit I have issues. Ask any of my ex-girlfriends and they'll tell you the same."

"Well, since none of them are around, how about *you* tell me."

Unfastening the twist tie on the cotton candy, he groaned. "What is it with women and talking? Can't you try to understand that sometimes I get a little worked up and leave it at—"

"Excuse me, but could I please get in there?" A middle-aged woman wearing thick glasses and a Tweety bird T-shirt nudged Jed away from the jogging suits. She looked at Annie. "I see you're buying two," the woman said. "Crazy how we have to snatch 'em all up so early. I've already got most of my Christmas shopping done."

"I know, me too," Annie said, putting the jackets back on the rack.

"You don't want those?" the lady asked.

I don't know what I want.

Five minutes earlier, Annie thought she would've been content with a new sweatsuit and an apology, but now she wanted more. For some reason, the argument back in the snack bar made her think of Troy. It reminded her of the way he'd seemed to deliberately pick fights, then gradually get louder and louder. Yelling and punching the walls and cabinet doors, then eventually punching or slapping her.

What happened at the snack bar was nothing compared to one of Troy's scenes, but—if only for an instant—it had returned her to memories better left forgotten.

"You go ahead," Annie said to the woman eyeing the jackets. "It's too miserable outside to even think about climbing into those."

Obviously, the woman didn't care, as she dove enthusiastically into the rack of clothes.

Keeping a tight grip on the stroller handle, Annie wove through the apparel maze to the purses.

"Does this mean you're going with me?" Jed asked, hot on her heels.

"This means I don't know what it means. Just that the last thing I want to do is stand around and chat about shopping. Jed, I want to—"

"Oh, my Lord! Walter, would you look at this! Triplets!" A white-haired woman with her stout husband in tow crouched over the babies, coochie-cooing and poking them to the point that Annie thought she might have to call for security.

Thankfully, Jed stepped in. "If I were you," he said in a stage whisper, "you might want to steer clear for your own protection. The babies bite."

"Oh, my." Eyes huge, the woman lurched back, clutching her chest. "I've never heard of such a thing. You should take them to a doctor right away."

As the couple wandered off whispering and glancing over their shoulders, Annie wanted to be mad at Jed for telling such an outrageous story, but she couldn't help cracking a smile. Not only had the man apologized, but he had brought her banana cotton candy, then made her laugh. Comparing him to Troy wasn't just unfair to Jed, it was ludicrous.

"You're awful," she said in a semi-serious tone.

"Thanks." He beamed with what she suspected was pride.

THEY WERE just past Wichita, playing a truly wretched kids' CD they'd found in the glove box when Annie dared to ask, "Ready to talk?"

"I thought we *were* talking."

"Sure. About whether or not those clouds on the horizon are producing rain. And whether to choose a McDonald's or Arby's or Taco Bell for our next pit stop. But near as I can tell, we still haven't touched on any important stuff."

Squirming in his seat, Jed said, "I thought you didn't like talking."

"Only on expensive cell phones."

He sighed.

"You told me to ask your exes about your…issues, but conveniently for you, none of them were lurking around the purse department just dying to spill your dirty secrets."

"What do you want to know?"

"Since you asked—" she said, propping her bare feet on the dash, ignoring his glare, "—how about telling me why you and your last girlfriend split up?"

Looking over at her, he said, "And you need to know all of this because…?"

"I put every dime I had on my condo. If we're going to be neighbors, I should know what types of floozies might be skulking around next door."

"*Floozies?* I'll have you know I only date the finest women the town of Pecan, Oklahoma, has to offer. I'm talking primo top-notch. Two former Miss Pecans, three rodeo queens and I nearly married my class's homecoming queen."

"That's an awful lot of royalty." Annie aimed a sweet grin his way. "No wonder you're proving to be a royal pain in the—"

"Watch it," he said. "There are tender ears present."

The kids' CD launched into a high-pitched, squealing rendition of "Row, Row, Row Your Boat."

"Wow." Annie winced.

In the back seat, all three babies gurgled and cooed.

"I take that back," Jed said. "Carry on. If they actually like this crap, those little ears of theirs can't be all that tender."

"All right, then, you're a royal—"

"Hey, whoa. I change my mind. *I'll* talk. Just don't ruin my Mary Sunshine image of you."

Fluffing her hair, Annie teased, "You think I'm perfect, huh?"

"Oh, I'm sure you have flaws in there somewhere."

"True, but back to yours…"

He tightened his grip on the wheel. "Well, the general consensus is that I'm too controlling."

"You?" Annie widened her eyes. "I never would've guessed."

"Hey, I'm trying to be serious here."

"Sorry," she said, her expression appropriately somber. "By all means, carry on."

"For instance, there was Beth. We were rocking along just fine at around the six-month mark when she announces out of nowhere that she's starting a night course at the community college. She wanted to learn cake-decorating. Well, I'm all for furthering one's education, so I was fine with that. My one request was, since her class didn't start until eight on Tuesday and Thursday nights, that I pick her up and drop her off. There'd been a mugging on campus just a few weeks earlier and I wanted to be sure she was safe."

"Oh, boy," Annie said.

"What? Even a year after the fact, I fail to see what's so bad about that."

"Nothing—if you were her husband. But Jed, if you two were just dating, she probably felt you were trying to control every aspect of her life. She probably thought you wanted to see if there were any hot guys in her class. Or that you'd think she was at some campus kegger, when she'd really been studying frosting techniques."

"Oh, please." Jed rolled his eyes. "First of all, it's a community college, so there aren't any keggers. And second of all, I didn't even *want* to be there. Hell, all I did was sit in the car and listen to all-sports talk radio.

It was a total bore, but as her boyfriend, I felt it was my responsibility to keep her safe."

"And you feel it's your responsibility to keep Patti safe."

"Exactly. See? You get it. Why couldn't Beth?"

"Did you ever try to explain your feelings to her instead of just asserting your need to control every situation?"

"Nah. Besides the subject of cake-decorating, she wasn't really big on talk."

"Talk about adorable. Sissy, come on up here and look at these three—make that *four*—cuties." The teen cashier at the small town's pizza joint cracked her gum and winked at Jed.

Jed pretended to be busy with his wallet. He'd already checked his messages, but maybe he should go and check them again until Annie got out of the bathroom.

A girl wearing a name tag that said "Sissy" approached the counter. "Ooh…they *are* cute." She didn't take her eyes off Jed. Great. How old were these two? *Maybe* sixteen?

"Want me to sit with you while you eat?" Sissy asked. "I can, you know, help you take care of your babies."

"Uh, thanks for the offer, but my *wife* should be out any—there you are, *honey*." His back to the counter, Jed winked at Annie. "Is one thin-crust Canadian bacon, black olive and pineapple all we need?"

"Except for my tea, *honey*. Did you order that?"

"Two iced teas," Jed said, relieved that Annie was playing along.

"Okay," the original cashier girl said. At her first sighting of Annie, Sissy went back to the kitchen. "Coming up."

Jed paid and headed for the booth where Annie had set up camp. Thankfully, it was far from the cashiers.

"Thanks," he said, setting their iced teas on the table before easing into the red vinyl seat across from Annie. "That was a mess."

"What was a mess, *honey?*"

"Those two girls. They were coming on to me. Both of them need to go home and play with their dolls."

"And stay away from real men like you?" She blew him a kiss.

"Anyone ever tell you that you've got a mile-long mean streak?"

Smiling, Annie shook her head. "Okay, Mr. Control. What would you have done if I hadn't been here?"

Jed grabbed five sugar packets, gave them a shake, then tore the tops off and dumped the contents into his tea.

"I'm waiting," Annie said. "Again."

"Truth? I probably would've made up some dumb excuse like I forgot my wallet and left. Stuff like that makes me uncomfortable. I never know what to say."

She put two sugars in her tea and stirred. "All you really need to do, Jed, is speak up. With Beth, you just needed to explain your feelings about wanting to keep her safe. And with those teenage girls, all you had to do was tell them politely but firmly that you weren't interested."

"Yeah, but what you don't seem to get that I don't *like* talking. Makes me itch." He scratched the back of his neck.

"You're so making that up."

Pia started to cry.

"Ah…" he said, removing her from her stroller seat. "Thank you, sweetie." He nuzzled the top of her fuzzy head, breathing in that good clean baby smell.

Which reminded him…

He searched the stroller pocket for the disinfectant wipes he'd picked up at Wal-Mart for just such an occasion. Taking one out, he began to wipe down the table.

"What are you doing?" Annie asked.

"Isn't it pretty clear? The last thing we need is for these babies to pick up a bug."

"But Jed, they're not even sitting at the table. And we're not going to eat here. We're only waiting until our order's ready to go."

"I'd rather be safe than sorry."

"Pia—" Annie said, reaching across the table for her chubby fists, "—it's my solemn vow to loosen up your uncle by the time this trip is over. Okay?"

The baby gurgled.

"There you go," Annie said. "At least someone in this crowd agrees with me."

"Yeah, well, the two guys think I'm pretty cool, so it's a three-two vote. I don't have to change a bit."

"NO, NO, NO..." Jed said. After checking his answering machine—still no messages—he now stood at the entrance of the World Famous Corn Museum, taking off the corn-husk hat not five seconds after Annie had put it on him. "I told you I'm only here to get the babies calmed down from their latest crying jag. Once they've had a few minutes to chill and forget how much they hate being in that van, we're gone," Jed warned.

"Fine, but what's the harm in having a little fun along the way?" She stood on her tiptoes to plop the hat back on his head. "Smile."

Before he could take it off again, she snapped his picture with the disposable camera she'd bought in the Corncob Hall of Gifts.

"What'd you have to do that for?" The hat was finally off and resting on the table she'd borrowed it from.

"You're the one who bought me this stupid shirt and insisted I put it on," Annie said. "Why shouldn't you look just as ridiculous?" She peered down at the nubby corncob on the white shirt. A caption across the top read I Hope To Be *Earring* From You Soon.

At first she hadn't gotten the joke.

Jed had been the one to explain. Ear of corn. *Earring* from you. *Hearing* from you. He bought her the shirt to remind her that *he* was the funny one. He'd even had the nerve to bring up her lame joke about his fried phone being served with ketchup or tartar sauce.

"And do you know why I wanted you to wear that shirt?" he asked. "Because I have a sense of humor and you don't."

"That is not true," she complained, waving her camera with one hand and jiggling a crying Ronnie with the other. "And I'll prove it by getting these pictures developed and showing them to everyone you know."

"That's not funny. That's blackmail." He tried to look gruff but couldn't hide the lingering smile in his eyes.

Slowly pushing the stroller by a floor-to-ceiling display of facts about corn, Jed whistled in amazement. "Did you know the biggest box of popcorn in the U.S. was over fifty-two feet long? Ten feet wide and ten feet deep? Wonder if it had butter?"

Ronnie wailed louder.

Jed gave his nephew a weary glare. "Have you given any thought to the schedule?" he asked Annie.

"A few more minutes of walking—and he'll calm right down."

Jed returned her reassuring smile with a skeptical scowl.

They walked past another exhibit—this one on the history of corn.

"Check it out," Jed said, pointing to a model village. "The earliest recorded windmills were in seventh century Persia, and they were used for grinding corn."

"Be careful," Annie said, elbowing his ribs. "Someone might think you're actually having fun."

He made a face at Annie, then continued to read each plaque on the remaining exhibits.

Ronnie kept crying.

At the end of the room stood an elderly woman volunteer, dressed in a long-skirted pioneer outfit. "Would you all care for a sample of early settler-style popcorn?"

Annie bit her lower lip.

Here it comes.

No doubt Jed would give the poor woman a lecture on how unsanitary her cooking method was.

"Yes, please," Jed said, accepting a paper sack from the woman, then turning to Annie. "Want one?" he asked an openmouthed Annie.

Even Ronnie must've been shocked by his uncle's surprisingly cordial behavior, as he'd quieted to a whimper.

"Sure," Annie said.

Behold...the power of corn.

He handed her his bag, then got another for himself.

After listening to a short lecture on how the treat was prepared, they moved on to a diorama of corn-husk dolls and different corn ceremonies performed by Native Americans.

Pausing in front of the door that led to the World's Largest Ear of Corn, he said, "After this build-up, I feel there should be a drumroll to mark such a momentous occasion. Here." He took the camera from her. "Park the stroller in front of the sign and I'll take your picture."

Eyebrows raised, Annie did as he'd asked and said, "So tell me, former Corn Scrooge, how is it that in the past fifteen minutes you've gone from corn-hater to corn-believer?"

"I never said I hated corn. I just don't like stopping. We're supposed to be keeping this show on the road. I have to admit, though, this has been educational."

"It wasn't supposed to be educational. Aside from calming Ronnie, this was just for fun. I wanted to loosen you up, and—"

Jed took a deep breath. "Can we please skip this latest attempt to analyze me and just see the corn?"

"As you wish."

He held open the door, but the stroller forced her in at an odd angle, sending her right under Jed's outstretched arm—right against his chest, into the danger zone of his all-male scent. Luckily, the sight before her was so awe inspiring, Annie just wanted to get a closer look.

Gripping Jed's hand in excitement, she said, "Have you ever seen anything like this?"

He shook his head. "Can't say I have. Annie, I've gotta tell you, I'm not sure why someone would build something like this, but I'm impressed."

Towering in the middle of a glass dome—surrounded by a thirty-foot circle of the greenest, most velvety-soft grass Annie had ever seen—stood what undoubtedly was the world's largest ear of corn in all its yellow glory. The thing was so tall, that in order to see the very top, Annie had to bend her head back so far it hurt.

Up in the cavernous room's rafters, barn swallows chirped.

"Damn," Jed said, hands braced on his hips. "How do you suppose they made this thing?"

It just so happened that the husband of the popcorn lady—he'd proudly informed Jed and Annie of this fact—was more than happy to fill them in on every riveting detail of the three-story plaster corncob's creation.

At the end of his tale, the man said, "Local legend has it that any couple passing through here must kiss each other under the Corncob Arbor for good luck in the rest of their travels."

Jed cleared his throat. "We're not, um, really a couple. We're just friends."

"Doesn't matter," the gray-haired man said. "If you don't kiss the lady, odds are you'll have a flat within twenty miles of the museum."

Annie's palms were sweaty against the vinyl stroller handle and her pulse all of the sudden wasn't so steady.

Would Jed really kiss her just because of some silly superstition?

Much to her secret shame, she hoped so!

While Annie scolded herself for even thinking such a thing, the old man eyed a gold pocket watch he'd taken out of the pocket of his faded overalls. "Four forty-five. You two better get on with it. The museum closes in fifteen minutes."

He wandered off, and Annie released her breath. "That was close."

"What?"

Playing it cool, she tucked her hair behind her ears. A nervous giggle spilled from her lips. "You know…"

"No, I really don't." He took a step closer.

"That thing about the kiss," she said, letting the inquisitive baby squeeze her index finger instead. "Could you believe how that guy was pressuring us? Jeez, the way he was going on, you'd think—"

And then all thinking stopped when Jed kissed her.

Soft, exquisitely warm, his lips met Annie's in a maddening maelstrom of emotion she couldn't begin to define—didn't *want* to define. She just wanted to appreciate it for the pleasant surprise it was.

When Jed stepped back, a grin playing about the corners of his mouth, she brought trembling fingers to her lips.

"You heard the man," he said. "It's a tradition. What else could I do? You don't want to spend another three hours at Wal-Mart waiting for our next tire change, do you?"

"Um…no. Of course not."

"Ready to get back on the road?" Jed asked, looking at his now sleeping nephew.

"Sure. I guess. But…shouldn't we talk?"

"Nah." He dropped his arm across her shoulders in such a way that she wasn't sure if he meant the gesture as a show of casual affection, intimacy or just plain friendship. Whatever it meant, Annie could scarcely breathe, so aware was she of his presence and the lingering taste of popcorn on her lips. "After all this excitement," he said, "I'm kind of sleepy," he said. "Would you mind driving while I catch a few z's?"

Chapter Six

Patti squeezed her eyes shut, praying for strength.

Howie had suffered an allergic reaction to one of his many medications, but his doctor promised he was improving.

Unfortunately, her husband's health was only the start of her problems. She'd tried calling Jed at least twenty times but kept getting his stupid machine or the voice mail on his cell.

Where was he?

What had he done with her babies?

"Oh, Howie," she whispered, clasping her sleeping husband's hand. "I wish you'd never taken that job. I wish I'd said let's sell our big house and the minivan and all my shoes and clothes. I'd be happy living in a tent right now if it meant the five of us could be together."

Hot tears sprang to her eyes.

She didn't bother to wipe them away.

What was the point?

Lately, her cheeks never seemed fully dry.

She leaned forward, resting her head against the soft white cotton blankets on Howie's bed. She held his hand to her cheek.

"Get better, sweetheart. I need you to help me find our babies."

ANNIE HAD PLENTY of experience driving vans.

The day-care van.

The preschool van.

So it wasn't the actual handling of the large vehicle that had her in such a tizzy.

Glancing at the passenger seat, the cause of her nervous stomach softly snored. How dare he kiss her like that and just fall asleep! Were they ever going to talk?

All three babies were snoozing, too.

Looking back at Jed, Annie realized that in spite of her frustration with him, he'd never looked better. At least in the short time she'd known him.

Even with his long legs folded beneath the dash. Even with his arms crossed and his head cocked at what couldn't be a comfortable angle, he still had a latent power she found devastatingly attractive. But with sleep had come peace and vulnerability—a trait she got the feeling he'd rather die than show during his waking hours.

And he'd trusted her enough to let her take the lead on their mission.

Any number of things could go wrong.

Another flat.

Engine trouble.

Taking the wrong road.

And yet he'd ignored all these possible disasters when he handed her the keys. Was she making progress in her quest to loosen him up? If so, that was great. But why did she care? It wasn't as if she'd reap any benefits from the new-and-improved Jed Hale once the trip was over.

Her lips tingled.

She turned up the air-conditioning and aimed the nearest vent toward her.

So what if she was thinking about the kiss?

And the crazy, wonderful, unexpected glimpse into what it would be like to come home from work every day and step into his open arms…

Why had he kissed her? Did he do it because their museum guide had goaded him into it?

If so, why did Annie feel sad that Jed hadn't kissed her for another reason?

An infinitely better reason.

Like the plain and simple fact that he'd found her impossible *not* to kiss!

"I DON'T SUPPOSE you know where we are?" Jed asked Annie, shading his eyes against the bright early-evening sun.

She finished strapping Pia into the stroller. "We're at the only two-story cow in the continental U.S. made entirely out of beer cans."

He groaned. "Please, God, tell me this isn't happening. Please tell me there isn't another beer-can cow somewhere outside the continental U.S."

"I wasn't going to stop," she said, "but then Pia laid one heck of a smelly egg. Since the place is open twenty-four/seven, according to the billboards I saw, and since it's got clean restrooms and changing tables, I figured we should stop. Why not stretch our legs and do a diaper change?"

"Sure," Jed said. It made complete sense. If you were out of your mind!

"Well?" she asked. "You coming?"

He rubbed his eyes with his thumb and forefinger, then climbed out of the van.

On the way to the giant fenced pen that held the cow, Jed noticed signs boasting live rattlesnakes and scorpions just inside, right along with peanut brittle and taffy.

"That's quite a combo, huh?" he said to his smiling companion. "I always enjoy having a good wad of taffy in my mouth when I'm checking out rattlesnakes."

Annie tugged at Jed's hair. "Quit being such a grouch. Can you imagine how long the creator of this cow must've worked?"

"Yeah, and can you imagine how he did it—drunk as a skunk on all that beer?"

"For that—" she gave his arm a pinch "—you're going to buy me taffy *and* peanut brittle. And we're going to keep to the schedule, so you're going to look at every single snake, scorpion and beer can in this building in under ten minutes."

"Wow," Annie said as they walked through the cow's belly. The freshly diapered babies happily gummed teething rings in their stroller. "This is even more impressive than I'd hoped. I never thought we'd be able to walk around inside. The giant corncob people need to step up their exhibit. This is much more fun than looking at it from the outside—even if it does smell like sour yeast."

"Yeah." Jed ran his fingers along the dusty row of cans that served—according to a hand-printed sign—as the cow's large intestine. "I was just thinking the same thing."

"You were not."

"Sure, I was." He almost succeeded in keeping a straight face. "Especially about improving the corncob. If the corncob people really want to draw in the masses, they should perform weddings in the cob, just like they do here."

"They do?" She wrinkled her nose.

"Why Annie Harnesberry, you haven't been reading all the signs?"

She stuck out her tongue.

"Look." He pointed to another handwritten sign. "It says so right here. For the low, low price of fifty bucks, we can get married by a real live justice of the peace and have a beer toast over white cupcakes and white-chocolate-covered pretzels."

"You're so making that up," Annie said, nudging him out of the way to get a better look.

"Puh-leeze. I'm not creative enough to make this stuff up."

Annie giggled. She read the sign, and sure enough, he was telling the truth.

"Does someone owe me an apology?"

"For what?"

"For accusing me of lying—right here in the sanctity of the beer-can cow's belly."

"No way."

"Yes, way," he said, easing her up against the cow's ka-thumping heart—which was actually beating, courtesy of a looped sound effect.

Annie fought for her next breath. Did he have any idea how much trouble this playful side of him caused? She couldn't think straight. Had she been too hasty in her decision to steer clear of *all* men?

"You know," he said, "there *is* one way we could remedy this situation."

"I, um—" Annie licked her lips "—didn't know we had a situation."

"Oh, yes, we do. It says so right here on this other sign."

"Which one?"

"The one that says it's bad luck if we don't kiss in here."

"Really?"

"Hey, I told the truth about the marriage ceremonies, didn't I?"

"Y-yes." Jed's breath was warm and sweet-smelling from all that taffy and peanut brittle they'd eaten while gawking at the snakes.

Annie knew kissing him would be a bad idea, but she couldn't help craving one more taste of his lips. Just one more kiss, and then she promised to stay away.

No more hair tugging.

No more pinches.

No more looking at him—well, maybe that was a little extreme, but—

Jed took the decision out of her hands by pressing his lips to hers in a decadent display of kissing perfection.

A contented moan caught in Annie's throat as she pressed herself against him, craving his touch, his strength. He urged her mouth open and she let him in, deepening their kiss with a thrilling sweep of tongues.

Pausing for air, Jed touched his forehead to hers. "We've got to get back on the road. What are you trying to do to me?"

"Me?" She laughed. "I was just thinking the same about you."

"So what're we going to do?"

"That's a no-brainer. First, we'll only make rest stops at places that don't encourage kissing. And second, if crying babies do force us to stop at places like that, we're forbidden to read the signs or listen to the buttin-ski guides."

"Sounds like a plan to me."

"Good." Annie smiled. "We agree."

"Definitely. I'm just going to need one more kiss."

"NOPE," Jed said an hour later at a standard-looking burger joint near Flamingo, Kansas. In a town named Flamingo, it was a wonder no enterprising local businessman in Pecan hadn't tried to make his fortune from a giant bird made of pink bubblegum wrappers. "We'll have to go someplace else."

"What do you mean someplace else?" Annie said above the roar of all three babies crying. "I realize you've been sleeping, but this is the only restaurant I've seen in a while. It might not be the cleanest, but…"

"Then you must not have been looking."

Annie turned away.

Could she have been more wrong about Jed's rehabilitation?

"Look how dirty this place is," he whispered in her ear, giving her chills when his warm breath settled around her. He gestured at an ant-covered scrap of hamburger bun that had fallen onto the muddy footprints at the base of the order counter.

Dust and a city of cobwebs lived on the silk ivy that decorated the cash register.

Ew. "Okay, but—"

"Can I take your order?" a twenty-something pregnant brunette asked above the babies' unanimous howl. She winced. "Dang. I'm glad I'm just having one. Bet you all never get any sleep."

Annie smiled politely. "Sometimes it's rough."

"You all know what you want?"

"Nothing, thank you," Jed said, taking hold of the stroller. "We've gotta get back on the road."

"Wait a minute," Annie said, fishing Pia out of the stroller. "I'll have a bag of corn chips and a bottled water."

"That's it?" the girl asked.

Annie nodded.

Jed scowled before storming outside.

Meeting him at the van a few minutes later, Annie said, "You didn't have to be rude. You could've ordered something that came prepackaged."

"Why?" he asked, taking both boys out of the stroller.

"Well…because it's polite."

"Right. And it's polite for whoever owns this joint to run such a messy ship? And what about when I was being polite back at the last fast-food place by pretending we were married so I wouldn't hurt those two girls' feelings? Remember how you were all for me standing my ground?"

"That's different," she said, kissing Pia's forehead.

"How?"

"Well…" *Because maybe when other females are attracted to you, I want you to be more vocal in your brush-offs!* Okay, so she was wrong. Her actions didn't make sense, but then, not much did these days. Especially her attraction to him. She cleared her throat. "You're missing my point."

"And what would that be?" he said over the collective crying of the babies.

She shot him a look. "Give me those two."

"I can calm them myself."

"Then might I suggest you do it?"

Annie opened the van's side door and slipped Pia into her seat. Her diaper was dry, so a bottle made her content.

She took Ronnie. He had a dirty diaper, which she changed on the passenger seat, then she gave him a bottle, too.

Richard had a dry diaper and didn't seem to be hungry, so she held him against her chest, humming one of the songs off of that awful kid's CD while nuzzling the top of his fuzzy head.

Jed slammed a pay phone back on its cradle and stalked off to pout beside the only tree within a hundred miles.

"Now what's the matter?" she asked, sandals crunching in the gravel parking lot.

"Nothing." He crossed his arms.

"Let me guess," she said. "Still no messages, and you can't stand it that I didn't blindly follow you out of the restaurant?"

A muscle twitched in his solidly clamped jaw.

"Bingo."

He sighed.

"Yahtzee."

"Stop," he said. "It's no secret that I'm usually the one running the show. But contrary to what your shade-tree psychiatrist brain evidently thinks, it's not because I like it, but because—" he looked sharply away, then said in a voice barely loud enough for her to hear "—that's the way it's always been."

"But it doesn't *have* to be," she said just as softly, stepping up behind him, curving her fingers around his arm. On the outside, he was steel, but on the inside, Annie suspected he was cream-filling soft. Hurt. What'd made him like that? Was it the death of his parents? Was it a result of Patti's rebellious teen years? Why did Annie have the uneasy feeling that there was something more? "Look, Jed, I know we're basically strangers, but in this case, maybe that's a good thing."

Jed laughed. "How so?"

"Well…"

She licked her lips, and it no longer mattered that she'd annoyed the hell out of him only minutes earlier.

The sun was setting in a fiery blaze across the western sky, and Jed was sick of fighting. What he really wanted was another kiss. His brief taste back at the beer-can cow hadn't been enough—not nearly enough.

"Maybe," she said cautiously, "you could try letting your guard down around me. I mean, since we're getting to know each other, you could practice trusting me the way I trust you."

"You trust me?"

"Duh. If I didn't, do you think I'd have left my home to come all this way with you?"

The sun streaked the sky with orange, yellow and violet. Pretty as that sunset was, it didn't hold a candle to the warm glow in Annie's eyes. The faint aroma of her floral perfume rose above the weary scent of baked earth.

Cupping Richard's head, Jed said, "You mean that, don't you?" He didn't meet Annie's probing gaze.

"I wouldn't have said it if I didn't."

"Okay, but *why* do you trust me? I'm a train wreck. Start to finish, I've bungled this entire mission. How can you feel anything for me but disgust?"

"This mission is nowhere near finished. And second, if you think you've bungled caring for the babies—remember that I've had years of training and experience. You've had a few days of sporadic babysitting. Give yourself a break, Jed. You can't expect to be an expert at everything."

Her words made sense.

His feelings didn't.

After his parents died—and even before that, when his little brother died—Jed had to be everything to everyone in some ludicrous attempt to make up for Ronnie's death.

He always had to be in control, because if he wasn't, he might lose something else. Someone else.

He had to save every helpless person from every fire.

He had to save his niece and nephews from their mother's refusal to grow up.

He *had* to do all of this, but suddenly, he no longer knew how. He was afraid, confused and overwhelmed. He'd been on his own for so long, and honestly, he was tired. Tired of always being in control. Of being the parent. Of never allowing himself to have fun.

The sun had set, and all that remained of the show was a faint orange glow.

Straightening his shoulders, he said to Annie, "We'd better get back on the road. Hand me the keys."

He'd be tired later.

Right now, he had to find his sister.

Chapter Seven

"Mmm…where are we?" Annie asked, rubbing her eyes, then stretching. Except for a yellow glow spilling in from a lone parking-lot light, the van was dark, chilly and brimming with the achingly sweet scents of babies and Jed.

"The Fill'er Up and Go station at mile marker four-seventeen. We need gas. This place opens at six."

The glowing green numbers on the dashboard clock read 2:37 a.m. "Oh."

"I'd keep driving, but the empty light came on a few miles back. There's an awful lot of nothing out here. I don't want to spend the next week walking if we run out of gas."

"Makes sense," she said through a yawn.

"Why don't you go back to sleep?" he said. "I've got this covered."

"Why don't we both sleep?"

"You go ahead. I don't want to risk snoozing through this place opening."

Annie snorted.

Even though she could've slept until Christmas, she said through another yawn, "I'm not all that tired, either."

"Isn't it a sin for preschool teachers to lie?"

She shrugged.

How could it be a sin to lie when that wicked-handsome smirk of his left her wide-awake and humming with awareness of how cramped the van was. And how all she'd have to do to once again be in his arms was lean a little to the left.

"You hungry?" Jed asked.

Loaded question. "Uh-huh. How about a ham-and-cheese omelet with hash browns and a side of pancakes?" Annie said.

"Mmm. I like your taste in breakfast."

"How far are we from Denver?"

"Three or four hours, give or take a few depending on how long the critters in back decide to sleep."

"It's pretty miraculous that they let us go this far without stopping."

"You don't think they're sick, do you?"

Annie sighed. "What I think is that they've finally worn themselves out from all the screaming they've done today."

"Don't you mean yesterday?"

Annie stuck out her tongue.

"Go back to sleep," he said. "I'll handle this."

"Why don't you let me?"

"Let you what?"

"Stay up. I'll make sure we're awake when the gas station opens."

"Haven't we already been over this?"

"Yes, but since I don't have a clue where your cabin is, you need to be alert to drive in the mountains. Therefore, it makes the most sense for you to sleep now, and me later."

"Yeah, but—"

"If you agree that I've made an excellent point, does that mean you actually relinquish a bit of your almighty control?"

He rubbed his whisker-stubbled jaw. "I didn't say that."

"True, but I dare you to deny that's what you felt."

"Why did I ever open the door that first day you showed up at my condo?"

"Hmm…" Annie beamed. "Could it be because you needed me?"

"You promise to wake me the second this place opens?"

Annie gave him the same look she would've given one of her preschool students hell-bent on licking the fingerpaints.

He closed his eyes. "See you in a few hours."

"JED?"

Annie shook him gently.

"Jed, you need to wake up. The station owner just turned on the pumps."

He slowly came round to find himself staring at a vision way better than that omelet he'd been craving earlier. How'd the woman manage to look so good wearing nothing on her face but a sweet smile?

"What time is it?" he asked.

"Six-thirty. The owner got a late start. He said he was up all night with his dachshund, Cocoa. She had three puppies."

"Oh." He straightened behind the wheel, then looked over his shoulders. The babies were gone. "Where—"

"Outside, they started fussing a little after five, so I got them out and walked them around."

"Why didn't you wake me? That could've been dangerous."

"What?"

"Walking around in the dark."

"What was going to get us? Other than that pack of yipping coyotes that finally knocked it off, there's not a whole lot to worry about out here."

"Yeah, well…" He opened his door and stuck his foot out. "You just should've woken me, that's all."

Annie jogged around to Jed's side of the van.

The babies were in their stroller, parked ten feet away on the store's covered porch. All three were drinking from their bottles.

"Face it," she said. "You can't stand the fact that we all survived the night without your help."

"That's crazy talk." Jed slipped his hand under his T-shirt and scratched his stomach. "I knew all along you'd be fine." Right. Which was why he'd faked sleep until accidentally falling into the real thing.

He had to get to his family cabin immediately. He couldn't let Annie get some softhearted notion that he needed a few more hours of sleep. He couldn't believe he'd gone and messed things up yet again by actually falling asleep. But Annie had done just as he'd asked and woken him when the gas pumps were turned on.

Only hours earlier, he'd wished for someone to lean on and here he'd found that person in the petite and perfect form of Miss Annie Harnesberry.

What else could he lean on her for?

Did he have the courage to try?

"Well?" she said, hands on her hips. "I'm waiting."

"For what?"

She coughed. "Your apology?"

Man, she looked good. The soft morning sun backlit her curls. Her eyes and skin glowed not from makeup, but from good health.

Just following his gut instinct without weighing the outcome of his actions, Jed pulled Annie in for a good-morning kiss. Looking at her and at his contented niece and nephews, it was suddenly a *good* morning.

They were safe, and in a matter of hours, he'd know his sister was safe.

At that point, he'd work on saving himself.

How?

By opening himself up to let Annie Harnesberry in.

"HEY, ANNIE?" This time Jed was shaking her awake.

She opened her eyes slowly and stretched. Her breasts strained against the thin cotton of her white corncob T-shirt. "Hi," she said with a lazy smile that tugged on his stomach and regions below.

"Hi." He smiled back. "We're in Denver. Still hungry for that omelet?"

She nodded. "Babies okay?"

"Freshly diapered and probably ready for their next meal. I got the formula can open, but I can never get the plastic liners to fit or fill them without making a mess. Would you mind doing that part?"

"Not at all." In fact, Annie was flattered he'd asked.

She made the bottles and the five of them walked toward the IHOP just off Interstate 70 that would take them into the mountains.

Pushing the stroller, Annie hung back while Jed opened the door, then ushered her inside with his hand warmly, solidly, on the small of her back.

The restaurant smelled heavenly—of sweet syrup, bacon and spicy sausage. Her stomach growled.

"How many?" the hostess asked.

"Five," Jed said.

"Will you be needing high chairs?"

He looked to Annie.

"No, thank you," Annie said.

The hostess grabbed two menus and showed them to a large corner booth well away from the other diners.

Once she'd taken their drink orders and left, Jed said,

"Think she's afraid of us dive-bombing her potential tips?"

Grinning, Annie said, "Maybe. But I like it better over here anyway." She doled out the bottles to the babies and tried to ignore the little voice that told her just how perfect this whole morning felt.

Jed's handsome face had been her first official sight of the day, and it was a good way to start. Something about the vibe between them now, about the way they seemed to be operating not as Jed and Annie, but as a team—a couple—felt right.

Not once had she felt like this with Troy or Conner. After what they'd put her through, she'd been afraid she'd never truly feel at ease with another man.

But here she was. Allowing Jed's smile to launch a whole new batch of cautious hopes. It wasn't fair of her to constantly urge him to share his woes when she hadn't opened up to him, either. But somehow she couldn't do it.

Not yet.

But soon.

Jed unfolded his napkin, used it to wipe the dribble from Ronnie's chin. "They must've been hungry."

"Has your sister introduced them to solid foods?"

Reddening, Jed feigned deep interest in a packet of sugar.

"Okay, mister. Spill it. What have you fed these guys that you weren't supposed to?"

"Nothing too exciting. Just a little ice cream at the zoo."

"And..."

"Maybe a few French fries."

"French fries? Jed! They could've choked!"

"I was right there. I mashed them with my fingers. I'm not letting anyone choke on my watch."

"That's it?"

"I, um, gave them a bit of a milkshake on the way home from the zoo. I just put a little in their bottles. And they had some licks of a dill pickle. I love 'em. I was curious if they would, too."

"No wonder they were fussy when I first showed up. Their stomachs probably hurt."

"From a few bites of people food?"

"You have to introduce solids into an infant's diet very slowly. You can't just start feeding them junk food."

"Yeah, well, I say that's how it should be done."

The waitress returned with two iced teas, then took their order for omelets and link sausage. They decided to share an order of pancakes.

The second after the food arrived, Pia and Richard got fussy.

Annie started to tend to them, but Jed said, "You go ahead and eat. I'm used to eating my food cold down at the station."

"You sure you don't mind?"

"Do I look like I mind?" he asked, a baby on each knee. He made goofy faces at both.

Pia giggled.

When Annie had been with Conner, he'd never once offered to let her eat while he took care of Sarah. She'd been the one to calm the baby, cut Clara's meat or make sure Ben used his napkin.

Looking back, Conner and Annie hadn't operated as a team at all. But considering how things had ended between them, was that really a surprise?

"Why so quiet?" Jed asked, bouncing the smiling duo on his knees.

"Just thinking."

"Oh, no. As much as you've made me spill my guts lately, don't think I'm letting you off that easy."

Annie fiddled with the syrup dispenser. "I was just comparing you to a guy I used to date—not that I think we're dating or anything."

"Sure."

"It's just that…" Suddenly, she couldn't seem to focus on anything but Jed's lips. On how tenderly he kissed. "He turned out not to be a very nice guy. And you…"

"Happen to be very nice?" His wide, welcoming smile warmed her inside and out.

"Yes," she said. "You're *very* nice, and probably very hungry. Here—" she held out her arms "—why don't you let me take those two."

"But you're not done."

Thinking of Conner had stolen her appetite. "Really," she said. "I'm full. You eat now. Then we'll get back on the road."

"Okay." He awkwardly stood to hand the babies off to Annie. In the exchange, his strong, warm fingers inadvertently brushed the sides of her breasts. The warmth of his breathy laugh, combined with the heat and goodness of the babies, confused her further.

She loved nothing more than infants.

What she couldn't do was mistake that love for her growing attraction to Jed. She wasn't interested in anything but her work and redecorating her condo. She didn't have room in her life—let alone, her aching heart—for another man.

It just wasn't time.

She hadn't had enough space to heal.

Jed kissed Pia on the top of her head, then Ronnie on top of his. He looked into Annie's eyes. Deeply. Thoroughly. Hungrily. No matter how hard she tried not to respond to his message, it was in plain view for all the world to see.

I like you, Annie Harnesberry.

Do you like me, too?

Without a word, he leaned forward and gently pressed his lips to hers.

"You taste sweet," he said. "Like blueberry syrup."

Terrified of what she might find next in his golden-brown eyes, she looked down.

"Now what's the matter?" he asked. "Didn't you want me to do that?"

She shook her head, then nodded. "I—I don't know."

Maybe the problem was that she'd very much wanted

him to do that. Despite knowing she had no business letting him this close.

And not just physically close.

A few kisses she could handle.

Maybe.

But emotionally?

Inside, she felt like melted cheese. Ooey and gooey and incapable of doing anything but molding herself to him. Was she attracted to *him* or to her idyllic picture of him? Was it the total package? The image of him as a loving father to three children? A loving partner to her?

The reality was that they were strangers.

She knew nothing about him.

He knew nothing about her.

So how come all she wanted to do was learn *everything?* She wanted to know him fully, spiritually, intimately. The way only a wife could.

"Annie?" He began to kiss her again, but she backed away. "Did I offend you?" he asked. "If I did, I'm sorry. I never meant to—"

"Please," she said, wanting to put her hand on his arm but struggling to restrain herself. "This kiss—all of them—have been nice. Better than nice. It's just that maybe we ought to present a platonic front for the babies."

Jed raised his eyebrows. "They're old enough to know about kissing?"

"No, but—" Both babies tucked close, she sat down.

"Go ahead and eat. You don't want your omelet getting any colder."

He took a bite. "I ticked you off, didn't I? I knew it."

"Knew what?"

"I came on too strong. You're probably right about us keeping it cool in front of the kids. But to give you fair warning—as soon as we pick up that no-good sister of mine, be prepared for some serious wooing."

AS THE MINIVAN GOBBLED the miles to Jed's cabin, Annie tried to sleep, but how could she with a loaded word like *wooing* between them?

Although she should've told Jed right then and there that she wasn't interested in dating anyone right now, she hadn't been able to get the words out of her mouth.

No, she wasn't interested in casual dating, but *wooing?*

That was an entirely different issue.

The old-fashioned word implied holding hands on long walks through Pecan's many parks. Rowboat rides at the city lake and bouquets of pink cabbage roses. Late-night phone conversations. Sharing popcorn at the movies…

"Just a couple more hours," Jed said, startling Annie from her daydream of what would happen *after* the movies.

She blushed. "Un-until what?"

He flashed her a funny look. "Are you okay?"

"Um, sure. Perfect." Especially since men hadn't figured out how to read female minds!

"Good. Anyway, I was just saying we should be at the cabin in about two hours."

"Great." They'd get Patti and at least have a chaperone for the trip home. But wait a minute. Annie's stomach lurched. Patti would've driven Jed's truck to the cabin. If Patti took her van and the babies home, that would leave Annie alone in the truck with Jed.

A misery-filled whimper came from Richard in the back.

Annie reached behind her and jiggled his seat. "Hang in there just a little longer."

Waaaah huh waaaaaaaaahh!

Jed sighed. "So close, and yet so far…"

Now Pia joined in.

Then Ronnie.

"Sorry," Annie said, giving Jed's shoulder a sympathetic pat that wasn't supposed to result in her palm tingling. "But it looks like our trip's been extended again."

"THIS IS BEAUTIFUL!" A few minutes later, Annie was rubbing baby heads while trying to catch a glimpse of the postcard-perfect view of snowcapped mountains cradling a shimmering lake.

There hadn't been anywhere to pull over on the steep interstate, but now they were approaching Dillon, a small town just north of Breckenridge.

Annie opened her window. It'd been mid-nineties in Denver, but it was in the seventies up here. The air smelled too good to be real. A blend of pine trees and water, earth and sun.

"Ooh!" Annie squealed. "Not only is this place gorgeous, but there's an outlet mall." Forget the mountains—check out the size of that Liz Claiborne store! "I wish we weren't in such a hurry. I could do some serious damage to my finances there."

"Watch it, buddy." Jed cursed under his breath when an SUV with camping gear piled on top cut him off, then did a U-turn. "Nice. Why don't you just skip the road and try driving on the median?"

"Goodbye, mall," Annie said. "Maybe we'll get to know each other next time I'm in town." If there ever was a next time.

Jed pulled into a gas station. "Shall we divide and conquer?"

"Sure. Want me to do babies or the gas?"

He sent a truly pained look over his shoulder into the angry pink-and-blue mob in the back seat. "Guess."

"All right, gang…" Annie unfastened her seat belt to climb into the back. "Looks like I drew the short straw, so work with me here."

She felt diapers. One—*ew*. Majorly loaded. The other two seemed okay. "Pia, dahling, let's get your latest surprise cleaned up."

She took the infant and changing pad to the second bench seat. Jed stood right outside the window pumping gas.

He waved.

Grinning, Annie stuck out her tongue.

He returned the favor.

She held up Pia and wiggled the baby.

Jed pressed his nose to the glass and made a silly face.

Eyelashes still wet from her recent tears, the baby girl giggled.

So did the big girl. "Your uncle's a charmer, isn't he?" she said softly, commencing with the business of unsnapping the baby's britches.

Pia cooed.

"Ah, so you agree?"

Luckily, Pia's brothers must've sensed their sister's change in mood, since they quieted, too.

"Agree with what?" Jed was back in the front seat.

"None of your beeswax. This is private girl stuff."

"You two making fun of me?"

"Maybe." Annie wiped the baby's bottom. Whew. For such a tiny bottom, it sure packed a potent punch.

"Girl," Jed said, "you stink."

Pia smiled.

"I'm gonna check for messages." He pointed to a nearby pay phone.

She waved him along.

Annie had to pause for a moment to counteract the affect of Jed's leaning over the seat in all his glory. Had there ever been a more gorgeous man?

Annie finished her task as quickly as possible—not so much to avoid the smell, but because being so close to Jed was just too darned hard. It made her think crazy things. Like how much fun it would be to cuddle up with him on rainy spring nights or snowy winter mornings.

When Jed returned and Pia was strapped back into her carrier, Annie asked, "Do you want me to drive?"

He shook his head. "I need something to do with my hands. I'm starting to feel antsy about what we might find."

"You don't think Patti's hurt, do you?"

"Nah. But I'm sure she's badly shaken. I know my sister. She needs me now—more than ever."

Chapter Eight

Patti eased her fingers around her husband's neck, hugging him as close as possible without causing him pain. "I've been so scared," she said.

"'Bout what?" His voice still scratchy from the tube they'd only recently removed from his throat, Howie laughed. "I'm a Mack truck. Nothing's gonna keep me away from you and our babies."

"I love you," she said, giving him another light squeeze.

"So," he asked, once she stepped back, "when are they springing me from this joint?"

"The doctor said she's going to move you out of ICU in a couple hours, then you'll probably be here at least another week on the regular floor."

"A week?" He tried to lift his arm to scratch his head, but it obviously hurt too much.

Patti did his scratching for him. "Once they get you into a regular room, I'll see if someone can wrangle me hair-washing supplies."

"Don't go to any trouble."

"Trouble?" She teared up but managed to give him a wavering smile. "Do you have any idea how awful the past few days have been?"

"Sorry."

"Just wait till you get healthy enough for me to pummel you, mister. *Then* you'll be sorry."

She hugged him again.

"I shouldn't have been driving that late. I'm just glad I only banged myself up and not someone else."

"Why were you driving, anyway?"

"To get to my next sales call ahead of schedule, which would get me back home to you and the babies ahead of schedule. Speaking of which, how are my angels?"

"Good question." Patti put her hands on her hips. "As soon as I finish giving you a piece of my mind for being so careless with yourself, that brother of mine is going to hear a word or two about the fine art of returning phone calls."

A MUSCLE IN Jed's jaw kept twitching, and it was bugging the hell out of him. Almost as much as the winter-ravaged dirt road that led to the cabin.

But the babies seemed to enjoy the constant bumping. They hadn't been so happy since he'd fed them all that ice cream at the zoo.

He gripped the wheel harder.

Man, he was nervous.

He didn't want to alarm Annie, but what if Patti was up here thinking about something drastic like committing suicide? Where had he failed in raising her? He'd done the best he could, but evidently that hadn't been anywhere near good enough.

The van hit a particularly nasty mudhole, jostling him all the way to his bones.

The babies gurgled happily.

"She's going to be fine," Annie said.

"What?"

"Your sister. She'll be okay. We'll probably find her lounging in the sun with a good book."

Jed's heart and mind reeled. He'd only known Annie a few days, and yet they were so in tune.

But were they really?

Was it the urgency of their situation that made him see things that weren't there?

"What's the first thing you'll say to her?" she asked.

He glanced at Annie and saw how she'd rested her arm on the open window. How the sun glinted golden off the fine hairs. How the cool, pine-scented mountain air ruffled her curls.

He was freaking out, but look at her.

So comfortable with her bare feet propped on the dash; he'd long since given up trying to cure her of the habit. She was so calm. So not at all like the chaotic images that flashed in his mind.

Patti with slit wrists.

Patti lifeless and overdosed.

Patti crumpled at the base of a cliff.

He pressed a hand to his forehead.

This had to stop. The whole control thing. He had to trust that Patti wasn't crazy, just hurting. He had to trust the woman beside him to help. Whatever they found, he wouldn't have to weather it alone.

As if reading his mind, Annie put her hand on his shoulder. Such a simple touch, but it meant the world.

"Thank you," he said, afraid to look at her.

"You're welcome."

Most women he'd known would have acted coy.

Thank you for what? they'd ask, wanting, *expecting* him to give more. Turning his thanks into a compliment-fishing expedition for themselves. And it wasn't that he didn't want to show how grateful he was, but at the moment, he lacked the emotional energy. Annie was different. She intrinsically understood his mental exhaustion. As soon as this ordeal was over, Jed planned to demonstrate in a hundred different ways how much her blind faith and trust in his mission had meant to him.

"Are we almost there?" she asked, removing her hand from his arm.

"Yeah," he said with a tight nod, pulse raging. "A few more turns and we'll come upon the lake, then the cabin."

"What's it like? The cabin?"

Bless her, she was trying to take his mind off the prospect of what they might find, hoping to ease his tension with small talk. Jed took her up on her offer. "It's pretty sparse. Log construction. One bedroom. And since it's inaccessible in the winter—the whole cabin, not just the bedroom—" he winked "—we just have a fireplace for heat."

"How about the important things? Electric? A flush toilet?"

Seeing the worried furrow on her forehead made him smile. "Yes, and yes. Although the power up here has a mind of its own."

She laughed. "Sounds like a beach house my parents used to rent."

They rounded the last curve, to be treated to the sight that never failed to stir his soul. On this cloudless day, the lake wasn't filled with water, but with midnight-blue diamonds. Most of the snow had melted from the mountains that embraced it, except for a few dirty white patches above the tree line.

Palms sweating, heart hammering, Jed turned another curve, the one leading to the cabin, to Patti. "Here we are."

"Where's your truck?" Annie asked as he pulled into the crude dirt trail that served as the driveway. "Think she parked around back?"

He turned off the van, frowning. "I have no idea. But then I can't imagine why she's even up here, so what do I know? Maybe she went to town for supplies?"

Annie unfastened her seat belt and lowered her feet from the dash. "I'll bet that's it."

Checking quickly in the back seat, Jed saw that all

three babies were wide-eyed and ready for action. Damn. Why couldn't they choose *now* to sleep?

"Go ahead," Jed's savior said. "I'll get this crowd into their stroller."

"No, let me help."

"Really. I'll be fine. You go on." There was her small hand on his shoulder again, her touch infusing him with strength.

He took a deep breath, then opened his door.

Half out of the van, he looked at Annie.

The corners of her lips were raised in a hopeful smile. "These guys'll be fine on their own for a few minutes. Want me to go with you?"

Swallowing hard, he nodded.

She checked the safety straps on the babies' carriers, gave them each a teething ring to gum and walked around front to meet him.

The place was eerily quiet.

A pair of mountain bluebirds tweeted and a light breeze shushed through the pines, but other than that, there was silence. It unnerved Jed, and he took Annie's hand. "My sister's loud. She always has the TV or radio on. Says it's background noise."

Annie squeezed his hand.

Together, they crunched up the path that led to the cabin's wide front porch. A couple of rockers usually sat out here. They stored them inside when they were gone.

The rockers weren't out. And that bothered him.

"It's beautiful here," Annie said. "How do you stand going home?"

"Once that first snow hits in September, it's easy enough to head down the mountain to places where it's still ninety."

They mounted the five steps.

Dust.

Yellow pine pollen.

Cobwebs.

Everywhere.

It was obvious that no one had been in or out of the cabin's front door in a while. All the shades were drawn, too.

Jed dug the cabin's key from the front pocket of his shorts. Reluctantly releasing Annie's hand, he took hold of the padlock on the door, then fit in the key.

It popped open with a click.

He took the lock from its faceplate and opened the creaking door.

"Patti?" he called into the darkness. "Sis? You in here?"

Nothing.

"Maybe, she's in town like you said." Annie crept up behind him.

"Yeah." But he knew from the faint smell of a long winter's dust that Patti hadn't been here at all.

He suddenly felt dizzy. Weak in his knees.

He set the lock on the dust-coated kitchen table, pulled out one of the chairs and sat before he fell down, pushing the heel of his hands against hot, stinging eyes.

He'd been so sure she'd be here. And if she wasn't at the cabin, where was she? Where else could she have gone?

Annie eased her arms around his neck, her breasts pressing against his back. She rested her cheek on top of his head. "We'll find her. I'll help."

"Where could she be, Annie? Where could she be?"

"I don't know," she said, voice scratchy, "but I promise you, Jed, we'll find her. There has to be some logical explanation. No woman in her right mind would up and leave three gorgeous babies who need her."

"That's just it," he said. "What if she *isn't* in her right mind? What if—"

"No. You're not going to think that way. It won't solve anything. Until we hear different, we're going to assume she's fine. Maybe she's lost or something."

"Yeah—it's the *or something* that gets me."

"Jed…"

"Okay, I get it. Positive thoughts. Now, let's lock this place up and get back on the road."

One of the babies started to cry.

"Are you kidding me?" Annie looked toward the van. "Jed, neither of us has slept more than a few hours for the past three days. The babies need to be out of their seats or the stroller for more than fifteen minutes at a time. I promise, we'll leave first thing in the morning, but please, let's just stay here for the night."

AN HOUR LATER, sweating from the effort of cleaning thick dust from every surface in the cabin, Jed asked,

"Are you sure you want to go through all this trouble for only one night?"

Annie glanced around the cabin with its lovably shabby brown sofa and chairs and the mismatched assortment of knickknacks that added up to a wonderfully eclectic home. Suddenly, she'd never been more sure of anything. She belonged here, with Jed, helping him find his sister.

"Yes," she said, putting her open palm on the cool, knotty-pine kitchen counter. "I feel kind of sorry for the place. It reminds me of some giant toy that used to be everyone's favorite, but then got abandoned for something better."

"Nah," Jed said, scrubbing the last of the pine-plank floor. "That wasn't the way it happened at all. This place will always be special. Back when Mom and Dad were alive, we used to spend entire summers up here. Me and my little brother—"

"I didn't know you had a little brother."

"I don't."

"But you just said…"

Instantly, Annie saw Jed's entire demeanor change. He went from gently scrubbing the floor to wiping it so hard that if he wasn't careful, he'd rub right through. "Forget what I said. Sometimes I have a really big mouth." He finished, then stood to fling the bucket of soapy water off the back porch.

Both doors to the cabin were open, as were all the windows, letting in a crisp-smelling breeze that should've aired out not only the cabin's musty-dusties, but their heads. It should have. So why did Annie get the feeling that Jed was hurting—and hiding more than ever?

"So after all we've shared, that's it? You're essentially telling me to mind my own business?"

He stood just inside the door, filling it with the breadth of his shoulders and chest. Backlit by the fading late-afternoon sun, Jed's face was a study in grim shadows. Annie wanted so badly to reach out to him, but how? He looked at her and stepped onto the small back porch.

Jed slipped his hands into his shorts pockets.

They should've gone to a motel. As much as he loved this place, it's obviously no good for him. Too many memories. And now that Patti wasn't here, there was too much pain.

And then there was Little Miss Walking Therapy Session. Without her saying a word, he could tell what she was thinking.

Really, Jed, you'll feel better if you open up.

Please, Jed, talk to me. Let me help.

Ha. What she refused to understand was that he was beyond help.

Life had dealt him some pretty crappy hands and that was just the way it was. But in life, you didn't have the luxury of folding or trying a new batch of cards.

In life, you get what you get and don't pitch a fit.

"Jed?"

"Dammit, Annie, why don't you understand that I don't *want* to talk about my dead brother?"

Eyes welling with tears, she brought her hands to her mouth. "All I was going to tell you was to look down. You have an admirer."

Embarrassed, ashamed, he did look down, only to get a much-deserved kick in the pants. Pia had escaped her makeshift playpen and now lay on her tummy, pretty-as-you-please, there beside his dusty Nikes.

She looked up at him, her innocence stealing his breath. How could he grouse about his lot in life with such a miracle right here in front of him?

Yes, his brother had died.

Yes, after that, his parents had drunk themselves into oblivion, dying in a senseless car wreck that had more to do with his father's inability to say no to vodka than anything else.

He scooped up Pia, hugging her fiercely.

He began to walk. Off the porch. Across the over-grown yard. Down to the lake's edge.

On the rocky shore, he allowed long-overdue tears to fall.

Tears for his mom and the red bandanna she'd worn over her hair up here at the cabin, because she didn't want any neighbors dropping in on her when she didn't look her best. Dad had always given her hell for that, considering their nearest neighbor was a good five miles down the road.

A twig crunched, and he hugged Pia harder, praying Annie wasn't standing behind him, witnessing his emotion.

He was a man, dammit.

A man totally in control of his life and surroundings.

From a few feet beside him, Annie said softly, "When I was little, I always dreamed of coming to a place like this. My parents were never all that keen on camping, though. They were more the Holiday Inn type. Remember how popular those used to be? For my eleventh birthday, my folks made sure they were back in town. They rented two rooms in the motel closest to where we lived. I got to invite three girls for a sleepover, and we spent practically the whole night splashing around in the indoor pool. My birthday's December fourteenth, so that was quite a treat. Birthday cake and poolside pizza with a grumpy sky threatening to snow. Boy, let me tell you, that party elevated my social status by a good mile. Anyway, this is a really nice place you've got here, mister. Not quite on par with a Holiday Inn, but I'm loving it just the same."

She put her hand on his shoulder, and that was his undoing.

He wanted to stay strong.

God, he wanted to stay strong, but he was too tired. He needed help. He needed Annie.

Turning to her, Pia still in his arms, he crushed Annie in a hug, the squirming baby between them.

Annie hugged him back as best she could, and they stood there for the longest time, hugging, not saying a word, while tears streamed down his cheeks.

This woman, this enigma, was so damned good for him.

Just when he thought he knew what she was going to say, Annie went and said the opposite. Just when he thought she'd scold him for not opening up, she pulled him in deeper into his heart, forcing him to open up whether he wanted to or not—at least to himself.

And how great was that? She didn't seem to care how he worked out his problems. She only cared that he did, and that he came back to her when he was done.

How could he have known her for a mere few days when it felt like a lifetime?

From where would he find the courage to tell her he had to stop seeing her when the time came to take her home?

For she'd become an addiction he would have to stop. He was no good for her. Always trying to be in control but failing.

She'd be much better off without him.

Trouble was, he got the feeling that without her, *he* might never be better again.

Chapter Nine

"Ugh." Annie lugged in the last awkward packs of diapers and wipes. On their way out of town, Jed had accused her of packing *waaaay* too many baby supplies, but since they were spending the night in a place that might as well be a thousand miles from the nearest Baby Depot, she was happy to have erred on the side of caution.

"Is that everything?" Jed asked on the porch, rubbing his lower back after setting down his heavy load of formula.

The creatures who drank all that formula were inside, indulging in their latest nap.

"I think so," Annie said. "Oh—what about our stuff? Want me to get it?"

"Nah. I'll handle it."

While he walked to the van, Annie stood on the porch, hands on the rail, enjoying the light conifer-scented breeze that brushed curls against her cheeks.

Wow, what a beautiful place.

Even though it was only six, the mountain's shadow crept into their sheltered valley, creating the illusion that it was later in the day. Time for a crackling fire in the stone hearth. For marshmallows and sharing stories.

The cabin and the land around it were magical.

Straight from a more innocent era, like those old Doris Day and Rock Hudson movies, where trouble was having one's hat blow off in a sudden wind.

She sighed. If only things weren't so complicated now. Jed was still worried about Patti. But what was Patti worried about? Was her marriage not as great as it seemed? Was she mired in an epic case of postpartum depression?

If *she* were Patti, Annie could've done a lot of thinking up here.

Annie swallowed painfully.

She had never felt so helpless as she had back there beside the lake, when Jed had poured out his soul with just one heartbreaking look into his eyes.

The man was eaten up inside, and she had no idea what to do.

Maybe that was why she got along so well with babies.

When they cried, all it took to fix them was the basics.

They wanted to be cleaned.

Fed.

Held.

Men, on the other hand, were a total mystery. Sure, she

and Jed had shared a few wonderful kisses, but that moment down by the lake, that had been much more intimate.

For just an instant, when he'd turned to her, reached out to her and only her for comfort, he'd been emotionally naked. She'd wanted to help him so badly, but how? Where did she begin to—

"That's the last of it," Jed said, clomping onto the porch, carrying their overnight bags.

"Looks like the cab light's still on. Want me to check it?"

He glanced over his shoulder toward the van. "Nah, I think it's just the angle of the sun."

Are you feeling better? she wanted to ask, but didn't have the nerve.

"What's for dinner?" Jed asked.

She blinked back hot tears.

So that was how it was going to be. He'd pretend what'd happened earlier hadn't happened at all, but because she couldn't bear to see him in that much pain again so soon, she'd let him go on pretending.

For now.

But not forever.

As his friend, she owed it to Jed to see him through his troubles with Patti, then help him handle a few of his own.

Isn't that considerate of you?

Like she didn't have problems of her own?

"Dinner, huh?" Thinking two could play the avoidance game—at least for one more night—Annie pasted on her brightest smile. "Dinner, huh? How about Canned Good Surprise followed by Stale Road Food?"

"Sounds good." He set the bags next to his feet and pulled her into his arms.

She rested her cheek against his chest and listened to his heartbeat, his breath.

What was happening between them?

What was her fascination with this man?

She hardly knew him, yet she felt as if she'd always known him.

Jed ran his fingers through her hair, and her throat ached with the tenderness of his touch. With her wish that life could be different. That love could be different. That neither had to hurt.

The pleasure and pain of it was devastating, and Annie squeezed him for all she was worth.

"I couldn't have done this without you," he said. "How can I thank you?"

Gazing up at him, tears pooling in her eyes, a smile playing on her lips, she said, "You just did."

"OUT WITH IT," Jed said several hours later in front of a crackling fire. "Where'd you learn how to whip up a meal like that out of nothing?"

Annie rolled her eyes while putting fresh socks on each baby. "It was just baked beans and canned ham. My grandmother taught me that crushed potato chip trick."

"Yeah, well…" He took the next baby on the assembly line and slipped Pia's chubby arms and legs into soft, pink pj's. "Next time you see her, tell her I like it."

"I will." She cradled Richard close and kissed him just above his ear. "You are so adorable. Do you have any idea what a heartbreaker you're going to be?"

"I can see it now," Jed said. "Us getting a call from his first-grade teacher telling us how he spends every recess chasing all the girls."

"Don't you mean Patti and Howie?" Annie asked.

"That's what I said." *Wasn't it?*

She looked so beautiful right now with her hair glowing in the firelight. She made him want his own family. His own wife, who'd never run out on him the way his flaky sister had. Annie would be a great mother. What else would she be good at?

"Do you have any idea how kissable you look?" he asked.

Laughing with eyes that were luminous and inviting, she shook her head.

"What do you think we should do about it?" he said, fingering one of her curls.

"Quit goofing around. We still have to get these guys and gal tucked in for the night."

"So? What's so tough about that?"

"You think they're going to fall asleep like magic?"

"A guy can dream, can't he?" Just as he'd dreamed of how his life might play out with her living in his home instead of next door....

"I've always liked dreams," Annie said softly.

Together, quietly, efficiently, in the coordinated motions of an old married couple, Jed helped Annie put the babies into the playpen he'd unearthed from the back of the van.

"They're perfect, aren't they?" she said, shyly reaching for his hand.

They'd set up the temporary crib in a corner of the bedroom where it was dark except for a milky swath of moonlight over three, blanket-wrapped angels.

Annie shivered. "Do you think they'll be warm enough in here?"

"Has anyone ever told you you worry too much?"

"Yes, but—"

Jed stopped her with a kiss.

Nothing fancy. He just wanted to show her how much he looked forward to the rest of their night.

She groaned, and the vibration of it against his chest pushed him over the edge. To hell with the restraint he'd been hanging on to.

He wanted her, needed her—*now*.

And he was so damned glad she felt the same.

Still holding hands, Annie led him into the living room, straight to the fire, then past the fire, then—what the…? "What are you doing with that Scrabble game?" Jed asked as she took it from a shelf. "I thought we were going to make out."

"How'd you get that idea?"

"Well, the way you kissed me back there, I assumed—"

She pressed her finger to his lips. "That's your biggest problem, Jed. I may worry too much, but you assume too much."

"NO WAY IS *muzjiks* a word."

"Sure it is," Annie said. "It's a plural variation of the spelling of *m-u-z-h-i-k*."

"Which is?"

She grinned. "A Russian peasant."

"Right. Should've known."

"One-hundred and twenty-eight points."

"I quit."

"But you haven't even played your first word."

"And I'm already so far behind, there's no way I could ever catch up. Can you think of a better reason to quit?"

"Now where's your competitive spirit? My grandmother and I play Scrabble all the time. She's so good, though, I have to study the *Scrabble Dictionary* on my lunch breaks."

"Well?" he asked, grabbing a handful of the Jiffy Pop popcorn they'd found above the fridge. "Do you win now?"

"I wish." She laughed. "I've *never* beaten her."

He sighed before placing d-o-r-k. "Has your grandma ever entered any tournaments?"

"Before her hip went bad, she was the Oklahoma state champ. But I don't think she's played much since her surgery."

"And what does that make you? Some kind of Scrabble hustler? Luring unsuspecting innocents such as me into—"

"Oh—" she said, nearly snorting her cocoa up her nose from laughing. "Let me get this straight. You—Mr. Kiss a Poor, Helpless Preschool Teacher in the stinky old belly of a beer-can cow—you are calling yourself an innocent?"

The size of his smile took her breath away. Had there ever been a handsomer man? A man she wanted to kiss as much as she wanted to kiss him? He was a mischievous boy and at the same time all man. A hard, muscled man. Although she knew better, she craved the taste of his delicious lips.

They each played five more words, and with every new draw of letter tiles, Annie grew more confused. What was she doing? Joking with him? Flirting? Was there something in the crisp, clear mountain air that made her forget her vows to stay clear of all men—and in particular, one as seemingly perfect as Jed?

They planned to head straight home in the morning. Once they got there, her good judgment would surely return, but until then, she was tired of being good. She was tired of playing Scrabble. She was tired of pretending she didn't find Jed incredibly attractive.

Still, tired as she was, she had to remember she was wary of nursing another broken heart. Already, no matter how hard she'd tried to fight it, her feelings for Jed went miles beyond what she'd ever felt for Conner or Troy.

Which was why, right now, before the fire glowed any softer, before they shared one more mug of cocoa, she needed to call it a night.

Feigning a yawn, she said, "I'm beat. Ready for bed?"

"Sure, but there's a problem."

"What?"

"Have you forgotten there's only one bed?"

"You can have it," she said. "I don't mind crashing on the sofa."

"Yeah, well, I mind. How about we share the bed?"

She folded the Scrabble board in half and let the tiles slide into the plastic bag they'd been stored in. "You think that's a good idea?"

"What's the matter?" he asked. "You don't trust me to keep my hands to myself?"

Oh, she trusted *him,* but she feared she couldn't trust herself. What if she rolled up against him in the middle of the night, basking in his warmth, his strength?

"Come on," he said, putting the screen in front of the dying fire. Finished, he held out his hand. "Let's get some sleep."

Not for the first time that day—or even that week— Annie followed her heart instead of her brain. Linking her fingers with Jed's, she let him lead her to bed.

"RISE AND SHINE, sleepyhead."

"Already?" Annie yawned.

Jed laughed and kissed her forehead. "Shoot, the

babies have already been up for hours. We're all fed and diapered and packed. All the van's missing is you."

"Why didn't you wake me?" she asked.

He trailed his finger so gently down her cheek she wasn't sure he'd touched her at all.

Hugging her down pillow, Annie recalled the long wonderful night she'd spent cuddled next to him. Had they met at a different time under different circumstances, maybe he'd still be in bed beside her.

"You looked so peaceful," he said. "I thought I'd just let you sleep."

Her stomach growled. She put her hands over it and blushed. "I don't suppose you brought breakfast?"

From the nightstand, he took a plate of the remaining peanut brittle they'd bought at the beer-can cow. "Sorry. This is all we had left—unless you have a craving for baked beans. In which case, I can open a fresh can."

She shook her head. "I love sweet stuff for breakfast. I'll pretend this is crunchy pastry."

"That's the spirit." He started to fold the playpen but didn't have much luck.

"Let me help." Annie said, slipping out from under the light down comforter that'd kept the chilly mountain night at bay.

In under a minute, she'd folded the playpen and slid it back into its carrying case.

Jed crossed his arms. "Woman, you delight in making me look bad, don't you?"

Grabbing her overnight bag on her way to the bathroom, she winked. "I'll never tell."

Five minutes later, she'd tucked her hair into a ponytail, slapped on a hat, brushed her teeth, washed her face, and changed into khaki shorts and a University of Oklahoma sweatshirt.

Back in the living room, she put her sneakers on. "Where are the babies?" she asked Jed as he stood in the front door. "I haven't even had a chance to hug them this morning."

"They're in their car seats. I have to admit, I'm a little antsy to get home."

"I'll bet by the time we get there, Patti's going to be the one worrying about you."

He took a deep breath. "I hope you're right—not that I want her to be worried, but—"

"I know."

The living room was gloomy with all the shades drawn and the dust covers back over the sofa and chairs. Had it really been just last night that the place had felt so inviting?

"Looks like you've thought of everything," Annie said. "Want me to strip the sheets off the bed? You probably shouldn't leave them on dirty."

"I grabbed them while you were in the bathroom."

"Okay…" She took one last look at the idyllic cabin she'd never see again. "I get the hint. Let's go."

Hand on the small of her back, Jed guided her from the house. She struggled to keep her composure.

Even though she hardly knew this guy, and had no emotional ties whatsoever to this run-down cabin, Annie knew she wouldn't forget the short time they'd shared.

Cooking that strange mix of canned foods for a dinner that'd actually tasted pretty good. Bathing the babies one by one in the chipped white porcelain sink. Laughing over Scrabble. Sharing that big old wrought-iron bed, and just as she'd feared, rolling into Jed's arms in the night. Only instead of hating it, she'd loved it. And she irrationally wished she could do all of it again.

Jed opened the van's passenger-side door for her.

Once in her seat, Annie promptly swung around to say good-morning to the three cuties chomping on teething rings. "I missed you," she said, touching the nearest hand.

"Believe me," Jed said, climbing into the seat beside her. "They missed you. I didn't think I'd ever get their diapers changed. Every time I thought I was finished, some wise guy—Richard—had to go again."

"Is he sick?" she asked, slipping off her sneakers to park her sock-covered feet in their usual position on the dash.

"If you're asking if he had the runs, his poop looked normal enough to me."

"That's good."

"I'll say. The last thing we need is a sick baby." He put the key in the ignition. "Ready?"

She nodded. "Let's go find your sister."

Apparently, the van had other ideas. Instead of turning over, the engine made a funny clicking sound, then nothing.

"Dammit," Jed said, thumping the heel of his hand against the wheel.

"What's wrong?"

Leaning his head back, he groaned. "Remember yesterday afternoon when you asked if the cab light was on?"

"Uh-huh."

"I'm guessing it was."

Chapter Ten

"Sheriff Franklin here," a man said over the phone. Static on the line made him sound far away.

"Ditch. Thank goodness I got you!"

"Patti Schmatti?"

She cleared her throat. "I go by Patricia now, thank you very much."

He chuckled. "Still touchy as ever, I see."

"Yes, and if you could actually see me, my scowl would tell you I'm calling for a serious reason. Jed's missing. And he's got my babies."

Ditch laughed. "Patti, Jed's not missing. He's looking for you. He asked me to check if you were at the cabin. I called to tell him you weren't, but I guess he decided to take matters into his own hands—as usual."

Fingering the pearls around her neck, Patti quickly told him what'd happened with Howie, and how he'd improved so much over the past twenty-four hours that his doctors were releasing him within the next few days. "I swear, sometimes I could throttle Jed," Patti said.

"Anyway, would you please, *please* run up to the cabin and see if he's there? And if he is…" She imagined herself throttling her brother. "Tell him to get my babies home ASAP."

"ARE YOU SURE you've got enough to drink?"

Jed brushed off Annie's latest offer of a second water bottle with a quick kiss to her cheek.

"It's only a twenty-something-mile hike back to the main road," he told her for the third time. "From there, it'll be easy to find a ride the rest of the way into town."

"Be careful," she said, cradling a blanket-wrapped Pia to her chest while Richard and Ronnie watched from their playpen, which had been set up temporarily on the sun-flooded front porch.

When he'd discovered the dead battery, Jed had felt like pitching the mother of all fits. But how could he when he had no one to blame for this latest disaster but himself?

"You be careful, too," he said. "The last thing we need is—"

"I know, I know," Annie mocked his deeper tone. "The last thing we need is a sick baby, or one getting hurt."

Despite himself, he grinned. "You'd better watch that sass."

She grinned right back. "Are you going to make me?"

"Don't tempt me," he said, "or I'll just stay here forever and we'll forget all our troubles and live off the land."

"Hmm…" She put her index finger to her lips. "It's tempting except for the fact that we're down to a one- or maybe two-day supply of diapers and formula, and since there's no cow handy and I'm not exactly…" She looked down and blushed. "Good grief." She landed a light swat to his arm. "Would you just get going?"

With one final wave, he set off down the road, tennis shoes crunching against frost-hardened dirt.

Even though he could see his breath, he was plenty warm once he got a half mile or so into his walk.

He'd made this hike for fun when he was a kid. Now, though, it was a major pain.

When Annie asked about that cab light, why hadn't he at least checked it? It would've taken only a second. Wasn't he the one who was supposed to be in control?

Right.

Not since the night his brother had died in that fire and he'd been helpless to save him had Jed felt more out of control.

And what kind of person was he wishing he could stay on this mountain with three adorable babies and one beautiful woman when Patti could be in serious trouble?

Not willing to answer his own questions, Jed marched on, losing himself in the scent of pines and the task at hand.

For now, he didn't have to worry about anything

more than putting one foot in front of the other. He had to get through this hike, then he'd worry about Patti. And after that he'd worry about how he wasn't nearly good enough for Annie. But at the same time, he wasn't nearly strong enough to let her go.

Not that he even had her.

But he wanted her.

And he wasn't just talking about sex.

Since meeting her, for the first time in years, he'd thought about what he wanted to do with the rest of his life.

He wasn't content to remain a bachelor forever, but with other women, he hadn't known how to tame the controlling beast inside him.

It was obviously no big problem for Annie that he wasn't always the most easygoing guy around, which made him think that despite his not deserving her, Annie saw something redeemable in him.

Knowing there might be light at the end of this latest tunnel quickened Jed's step.

The sooner he got to town, the sooner he'd get back to Annie.

Famous last words.

Whether it was the altitude or that he wasn't fit as he used to be, Jed felt like hurling, passing out or just plain collapsing—not necessarily in that order. Perhaps all that running hadn't been such a good idea.

Making matters worse, he'd stumbled a ways back

and dropped his water bottle. Just his rotten luck that it fell on a jagged rock that had punctured the plastic. He'd never admit it to her, but Annie had been right. He should've taken a second bottle.

He was hunched over, hands braced on his knees, when he heard the best sound ever—an engine headed his way.

Glory, freakin' be.

He glanced up to see his good friend Ditch's squad car. "Jed?" Ditch called from his window. "What the hell are you doing?"

"What's it look like I'm doing?"

Ditch laughed. "Having a coronary on the side of my road. Get in."

"Thanks." Jed climbed in on the passenger side.

Reaching into a small cooler between the seats, Ditch pulled out a grape pop. "Want one?" he asked, holding out the dripping can.

"You still drinking this crap?"

"Are you turning me down?" Ditch asked, snatching it back.

"Not on your life." Jed took the pop and opened it. "At this point, I'd be happy to drink motor oil as long as it's cold." He finished half the can in one gulp. "Damn lucky coincidence running into you. What're you doing up here?"

"It's no coincidence," Ditch said, putting the car in gear and starting back up the mountain. "I heard from Patti this morning."

Jed choked on his pop. "As in my sister, Patti?"

"One and the same."

"Did she happen to tell you where the hell she ran off to, so I can hightail it over there to—"

"Whoa, bud. Cool down. It isn't what you think."

"Oh, that she ran off on her kids like—"

"Cool it, man. Like I told you, it's not what you think."

"Well, then, what is it? Did she go off with another man? She—"

"She's been in the hospital."

Jed's stomach fisted. "What happened? Is she all right?"

"It's not her, it's Howie. He was trying to make it to his next town ahead of schedule when he fell asleep and slammed into an oak. Patti said she tried to call, but couldn't get you. Then something happened with the hospital phone lines. Anyway, she's safe. Howie's on the mend. And she's been beside herself trying to find out if her babies are all right." Eyeing Jed for a moment, Ditch said, "Look, knowing Patti's reputation, I took the liberty of contacting your pal Ferris in Pecan and her story checks out. He's been trying to call you because he found your truck at the Tulsa airport. Jed, she was telling the truth. This time she wasn't just running away."

Jed brought his hand to his aching forehead.

No.

No way this was happening.

No way could he have screwed up this badly.

Jed thumped his head against his window.

"So let me get this straight…" Ditch laughed so hard he started to snort. "You *had* to find her yourself, right? Didn't trust anyone else to do the job?"

While his supposed friend continued to howl, Jed turned away.

"Well, one good thing came out of it. At least I got to see you. It's been a while. Marthe'll be thrilled. 'Course you'll have to let her cook for you tonight. You know what a kick she gets out of feeding the world."

"It's not just me I dragged up here," Jed said, head and heart pounding with regret.

"Well, sure, the babies are invited, too. Marthe would rather see them than either one of us, anyway."

"There's someone else," Jed said.

"Oh, yeah?" Jed's old friend shot him a sideways glance. "Well? Who? Did you hire some grandma to help out with the triplets?"

I *wish.* "Her name's Annie. She's a neighbor."

"Oh? Grandma-type neighbor or hot neighbor?"

Hot. Very hot.

Jed shrugged. "*Just* a neighbor."

Ditch started in again with his snorting. "*That* kind of neighbor, huh? Damn, looks like for once we're going to have some decent entertainment round here."

ANNIE'S NEW FRIEND Marthe put her feet up on the porch rail and sighed. "It's sure good to have Jed back. Ditch never volunteers to do the dishes."

"Oh?" Annie said, taking a swig of the peach wine cooler Marthe had brought. Marthe had indigestion and was drinking Sprite.

"If you ask me," Marthe said. "He's out to impress you."

"No, Jed's just being polite."

Laughing, Marthe patted Annie's knee. "I took you for smarter than that. Nope, I've known Jed all my life, and he's never been that keen on housework. Billy!" Marthe shouted to her seven-year-old son. "Get off that stump right now!"

He didn't.

"Excuse me," Marthe said. "Time to get mean before he falls and we spend the rest of the night in the nearest emergency room."

While Marthe stomped off the porch and through the small forest that was the front yard, Annie took another sip of her wine.

No, Jed wasn't out to impress her with his offer to clean up after dinner. He was trying to compensate for dragging her all the way up here for nothing. Little did he know, this was the best time she'd had in years. The day had turned out to be truly enjoyable once she'd heard that Patti and her husband were okay.

Soon enough, they'd have time to head home.

Soon, she'd start her new job and spend her evenings redecorating instead of listening to Jed's booming laugh—the one now drifting through the cabin's open door.

What a wonderful sound.

The whole night had been filled with laughter, and this new playful side of Jed's personality was potent. Was it the norm for him? Or was he on an artificial high after hearing that his sister was safe?

Marthe, Billy in tow, walked back up onto the porch. "You get inside and stay there until I say you can come out."

"But, Mom, I—"

"Now," Marthe said, hands on her hips. "I already have a stomachache. The last thing I need is to stand here arguing with you."

Chin to his chest, the little boy did as he was told.

A wink, followed by a quick grin at Annie, showed the drill-sergeant mom was all bark and no bite. "Ditch is so lax in discipline. Seems like I'm always the bad guy."

"Overall, though, both of your kids seem very well behaved. Especially Kayla. I can't believe the way she's looked after the babies all night."

"Yeah, she loves little ones. Ditch and I have thought about having more, but financially, it's all we can do to keep clothes on two. I'm not sure how we'll manage when they start college. You and Jed ever talk about having your own brood?"

Annie was glad she'd already swallowed before hearing Marthe's question, or the shock of it would've left her choking on peach-wine cooler. "W-we hardly know each other. We're just neighbors."

"That may be," Marthe said, "but I've got a sixth sense about these things. You two are in it for the long haul."

Not wanting to argue with Marthe, Annie decided to let her think whatever she liked. Marthe might have a sixth sense, but Annie had a keen sense of realism.

"I need a back rub after all that hard work," Ditch said, strolling onto the porch, Jed behind him.

"Is that my cue?" Marthe asked, casting her husband an indulgent smile.

She stood, and took Ditch by the hand to guide him to her chair. Once he was seated, she began to rub his shoulders and neck.

Ditch closed his eyes and moaned.

Annie turned away. Somehow, the scene felt too intimate for her to watch. They were so obviously in love that it almost hurt to look at them.

She wanted what they had.

Jed stepped up beside Annie and she was suddenly very aware of his sheer size. He smelled of lemony dishwashing liquid and faintly of Marthe's barbecue ribs. "Do you need a back rub?" he knelt to ask, his breath tickling Annie's ear.

She shivered.

"Cold?"

No. More like disturbingly aware. No other man had ever made her feel such pleasure just by asking a question.

If only she didn't doubt his intentions. If only she had the courage to ask him if what he'd said back at the giant corncob, about wanting to date her after they got home, was true. What if he said yes? And what if he didn't want to wait until they got home? What if tonight, right here in this cabin, he kissed her long and leisurely until her toes curled with pleasure?

Had she really praised herself for being a realist a few minutes ago?

"Mom!" Billy cried. "Can I come out yet?"

Marthe laughed. "Oops."

"You'd make a lousy cop," her husband teased. "Imagine if you treated prisoners as badly as our poor kids."

"Oh, right," she said, smacking him on his red-haired head. "Like the kids and I haven't spent all afternoon decorating cookies for the Founder's Day parade. And yesterday, I drove that cherub-cheeked little demon into Denver so he could have the right baseball cleats."

"Watch out, Jed." Ditch laughed. "Protect your bachelorhood at all costs. Or else you'll end up like me— broke and completely whipped."

"I'll keep that in mind," Jed said, laughing too as he and Marthe went inside.

"Mom?" Kayla met her mother by the door. "Can we *pleeeeeease* keep the babies? They'll be good, and I promise to do everything for them. Hailey could come over and we could babysit together. It'd be good practice for when we're allowed to babysit by ourselves."

"Fine with me," Marthe said, "but you'll have to ask Jed. He's their temporary daddy."

Kayla turned her sweet smile and big brown eyes on Jed, and he was a goner. "Are you sure that's what you want to do?" He asked. "They're a real handful."

She nodded solemnly.

Marthe winked, and said, "Besides, now that you don't have to get back right away, this'll give you two a much-needed breather before the trek home. Why don't we take the van. We'll stop by the store on the way home and get you stocked up on baby supplies. Tomorrow, all you have to do is drop by the house, grab the triplets, and then you'll be ready to go."

Jed scratched his head. "Sounds like a great plan, but I still say it's an awful lot of work. What do you think, Annie?"

Annie gulped.

What do I think? That a night alone with you in this romantic setting could be trouble. "Um, maybe the triplets ought to stay here? They've got so much stuff."

"Then I guess it's a good thing Kayla and I brought our men," Marthe said. "Billy, Ditch, help us load the van."

Chapter Eleven

"That was nice," Annie said after waving goodbye to their company. She carried the cup Billy had used for his soda to the sink.

"Yeah. Ditch and Marthe are good people." He shook his head. "I can't believe how those kids have grown."

"That Kayla sure is a cutie." She turned on the warm water, holding the cup under the flow while running a soapy dishrag around the rim. In a pitiful few seconds, the cup was rinsed and dried and tucked beside its friends in the cabinet, leaving Annie not quite sure what to do with her hands.

Jed knelt to grab a napkin from the floor. He put it in the paper sack they'd set up for trash. "Kind of strange around here without the babies, isn't it?"

Yeah, Annie thought with a pang of sadness.

Look at us.

Without the triplets between them, they didn't have anything in common. Nothing to talk about. Did that mean they weren't supposed to be more than friends?

Jed chuckled. "Let me rephrase that. Strange in a *good* way. We never get the chance to finish a conversation with my niece and nephews around. When you were telling me this afternoon about your plans to decorate your new classroom like a giant underwater scene. I was going to say how cool that sounded but Ronnie interrupted, demanding his diaper be changed that second."

"Really?" Annie said, busying her fingers with a stray curl. "I thought you just didn't know a polite way to tell me my idea stinks."

"Heck, no." He braced his palms on the opposite side of the island. "In fact, if you don't mind, I'd like to help out. I'm pretty good with tools. Maybe I could build one of those reading lofts you sometimes see in kindergarten classrooms. We could paint it to look like a coral cavern underneath."

"Th-that would be great," Annie said, charmed anew. How come every time she thought she had their relationship—or lack thereof—figured out, the man had to go and confuse her?

Jed flashed Annie a smile so handsome that she had trouble finding her next breath. "So?" he asked. "You gonna give me another shot at reclaiming my Scrabble honor?"

"Sure you're up for it?" she teased.

"Damn straight. Last night, I didn't even try. Tonight, you're toast."

AN HOUR LATER, seated in front of a crackling fire, Jed groaned. "Please tell me I didn't just get whomped again."

Grinning as she slid the letter tiles into their bag, Annie said, "If that's what you want to hear, that's what I'll tell you. But there's no way you'll ever beat me. I've got too much of my grandmother's Scrabble blood pumping through my veins."

He rolled his eyes, then surprised her by taking her hand. "Thanks," he said, his voice a throatier version of its normal timbre.

"For what?" She gave his hand a squeeze, releasing it to tuck the game board into the box.

"For making me forget—at least for the past hour— what an unbelievable fool I've been."

She made a face. "I wouldn't go that far. Over-the-top concerned, sure, but not foolish, Jed. You love your sister. Because of that love, you put your own life on hold to search for her. What's wrong with that?"

"Anyone ever tell you you're too good to be true?"

"Nope. But I do get told to mind my own business. To get my own life. My girlfriends at the school where I used to work got tired of me always giving my two cents' worth about their relationships with their husbands or how to discipline their kids when I didn't have either."

The fact that she knew almost everything about Jed, but had told him precious little about her own rocky past, gnawed at her conscience. He deserved to know. *Everything.* But she couldn't open up. Not quite yet.

Jed brought her hand to his mouth, palm up, and kissed the sensitive center.

She shivered inside.

"Do you ever want any kids, or a husband?" he asked, his warm breath on her hand causing even more internal distress.

She nodded. "It'd be awfully lonely living the rest of my life alone."

"What kind of guys do you date?"

"What is this?" she asked with an easy smile. "The Dating Inquisition?"

"Sorry. Guess that's just my knuckleheaded way of asking if I'm your type."

"Stop!"

"What?"

"Putting yourself down. For the record, yes. At times on this trip—namely in unsanitary fast-food restaurants—you got a little domineering. But aside from that, you've been thoughtful and caring and—" She stopped just short of adding wickedly handsome to the list.

She traced the worried furrow of his brows. "Let it go, Jed. Whatever's bothering you about Patti, forget it. I can see it's still eating you up inside."

"That's just it," he said, leaning against the sofa and staring into the fire. "Sometimes I'm afraid that this compulsion to control everything is all I have... Remember how I mentioned that our house burned down when I was a kid?"

"Yes," she said quietly.

"I was sound asleep when Mom screamed at me to get up. Not many people had smoke detectors in those days, but my parents woke up because Mom had bad asthma and the smoke made her cough.

"Their room was at the top of the stairs. Next came Patti's, then mine, and my little brother Ronnie's room was all the way at the end of the hall. By the time Mom grabbed Patti, she was coughing so hard she could hardly breathe. Dad yelled at her to get outside. Dad got me and held my hand till we were outside. There was snow on the ground and I can still feel the icy-wet ground soaking my socks."

"Oh, Jed..." Annie placed her hand over her mouth. "I'm so sorry."

"Oh." He laughed sharply. "That's nothing. It gets better. After leaving me with Mom and Patti, Dad ran back in to get Ronnie, but it was too late. The stairs were gone. The firemen weren't there yet. I remember hearing their sirens, but they were still far away. Dad ran around the side of the house to get a ladder and prop it up against Ronnie's window, but the ladder was buried under the snow. He dug and dug screaming for me to help. I did the best I could, but it wasn't enough."

Jed started to cry.

Tears hadn't helped him that night any more than they did now.

"I kept waiting to hear my little brother crying. He was only four. He cried a lot. But the only sound was the wail of those sirens. By the time firemen got there and busted through Ronnie's bedroom window, he was dead. Smoke got him—not fire. I just stood there, staring. Dad said, 'Why didn't you help me dig, Jed? Why didn't you help?'"

Annie sat on the floor beside him, slipping her arm around him. "What a horrible thing to say. But Jed, you know your father didn't mean it. He must've been out of his mind with grief."

"Yeah, that's what he said later when Mom yelled at him, but it didn't matter. It was already too late. Things were never the same after that. The house I'd lived in my whole life was gone—along with all the memories of good times. Dad started drinking. Mom's asthma got worse. I began to help around the house more and more until I felt like I was the parent and my folks were the kids. Hell, maybe a part of me was a little relieved the night they died. How sick is that? At least after they were gone, I stopped having to make excuses for them to Patti. I used to tell her Dad was too sick to come to her softball games when, in reality, he was soused. I didn't even tell him about her games for fear he'd embarrass her in front of her friends. And Mom…she could've tried to get better, but she wouldn't take her medicine. I wanted so badly to fix it. Them. Me. To make everything better. Nice. Happy. The way it was before Ronnie died.

"I thought that if I worked hard enough, I could bend life to my will. For a while, with Patti, it worked. But everything went bad when she hit her teens. I wasn't her parent. Tupac was. Hellhammer and Black Flag. I was just the guy who kept her from doing what she wanted. The more I tried to control her, the more out of control she got. That's why I came up here now. I had to drag her back. I had to at least try." He covered his face with his hands. "That's the only way I stay sane."

Annie sighed before pulling him into her arms. "I'm so sorry," she said, stroking his hair. "So, so sorry."

"I didn't tell you so you'd feel sorry for me," he said. "I can handle it. All of it. I just need a breather, you know? Time to catch my breath."

"I know, Jed, I know." Cradling his face in her hands, she kissed his forehead and cheeks and nose. "What you have to realize is that Patti's a grown woman now, not a wild teen. No matter how hard you try, you can't control her any more than you can the weather or a flat tire or a dead battery." Smoothing his hair back from his forehead, she said, "Once you understand that no one—not even a man as strong as you—can control every aspect of his life, you might be able to conquer your fear of losing control."

"If only it was that easy," Jed said with a pained laugh. "Do you think I haven't tried?"

"Listen," she said, watching his tearstained face. "As an experiment, try controlling me like you have every other aspect of your life."

He shook his head. "I don't know what you mean. I wouldn't do that to you. I couldn't. I respect you too much."

"That's good news," she said with a wavery smile, tears pooling in her eyes at the fear that she might lose her nerve and not follow through on the outrageous act she had in mind. "Because if you try to stop me, we won't have nearly as much fun."

She unfastened the top button of her blouse, then the next and the next.

He groaned. "Annie, please. You don't know what you're doing. I didn't tell you all this to make you think I'm some charity case."

"Did I say you had?"

"No, but—"

She pressed her lips to his—hard. She forced his mouth open, nipped at his tongue. She was unbuttoning the rest of her shirt when he put his hands on hers.

She thought he was helping at first, but then she saw he actually intended to stop her.

"Good boy," she said softly.

"Excuse me?"

"You just proved my point. The experiment failed. I want to make love to you, Jed. No matter how hard you try, you can't control that."

"Are you *sure* this is what you want to do?"

"You don't want me to have my way with you?"

For the first time in a while, he grinned. "I didn't say that. I'm just, you know, not accustomed to a woman taking the lead."

"Yeah, well, get used to it. I can't believe I'm admitting this, but Jed Hale, from the first moment I saw you, all I could think of was how good it would feel to be held in your arms. I've got a past, too. And deep down, something's telling me that only a man as honorable as you can heal me. Make me whole."

Cupping her face, he asked, "What happened?"

She was suddenly laughing—and crying. Kissing him. Burying her fingers in his hair. "Heal me, Jed. Please."

Aside from the time it took to tug off his T-shirt and help Annie lose her top, Jed never broke her stare. At least not before muttering, "Oh, crap."

"What?"

"Protection. I mean, I know I'm clean, but I'm not the kind of guy who carries condoms in my wallet."

"It's okay," she said. "I'm on the pill—and I'm also *clean*." Feet tucked beneath her, she reached around to her back to unfasten her bra. When her breasts were free, she watched in wonder as Jed sucked in his breath.

"If I'd had any idea you were hiding all that under those T-shirts of yours," he said, "I would've seen about getting them off you a long time ago."

She giggled. "We've only known each other a few days."

"Right. A few *agonizing* days." He nuzzled her neck, starting a delicious new batch of shivers. "You think I haven't been wanting you? If we hadn't been saddled with my sister's kids, I would've put the moves on you in that smelly old beer-can cow."

"You did."

"Did what?"

"Put moves on me in there."

"Are you talking about that measly kiss? Honey, that was nothing. You're not going to believe what else I have in store."

"Mmm...I can't wait."

And she didn't have to.

Jed stood, then scooped her into his arms, carrying her to the bedroom where he eased her onto the bed and settled beside her. "Wanna know why I was up so early this morning?"

She nodded.

"Because lying next to you got me so damned hot I thought I was gonna explode. It was easier to just get up than lie there rock-hard."

"Wanna know why I didn't want to wake up this morning?" she asked, straddling his waist, then raining kisses on his chest.

"Oh, hell, yeah."

"Because I wanted to snuggle up next to you, but knew I shouldn't."

"Why not?"

"I wasn't sure if you liked me for *me,* or if you were afraid you couldn't handle the babies without me."

"Are you crazy?" Jed asked, flipping Annie over so that he was on top. The room had been dark, but he switched on a bedside lamp. "I want you to look into my eyes when I say this. Annie Harnesberry, you are the *total* package. Sweet, gorgeous, funny. The fact that you also happen to be great with kids is just a bonus."

"Really?" she said, scarcely able to trust her ears. "Do you mean that?"

"Hey," he said, toying with one of her curls. "What's this sudden insecurity? Does this have to do with the creeps you used to date?"

She nodded.

"Well, you're with me now. And I promise, you'll never have to worry about another single thing ever again."

His promise was another attempt to control matters that were completely out of his control, but for the moment, she chose to ignore his backsliding. Besides, it was kind of hard to scold him when his touch made it impossible to even think.

JED WOKE to a stream of sunlight warming his legs and a wild, wonderful woman warming his chest. Damn, how such a small person managed to hog such a large bed and all the covers he'd never know—not that he was complaining. As far as he was concerned, after the night they'd just shared, she could have anything she wanted. Including his heart.

He rubbed a night's worth of stubble on his chin. Was he actually thinking the "L" word after only a few days?

He frowned.

Probably not. But in the meantime, he wouldn't fight it.

For much longer than he cared to remember, he'd presented a happy face to everyone, while Patti's antics shredded him up inside. Now, after hearing Annie's take on the matter, he realized he'd given his sister all he had to give. And that was enough. She hadn't run off and abandoned her children like he'd originally feared. She'd gone off to nurse her sick husband.

How could he fault her for that?

The beauty beside him stirred.

"Good morning," he said, running his open palm along the rise and fall of her back.

"Yes, it is." She grinned.

Good Lord, what the woman did to him with just that smile. Part of him wanted to stay up here forever, never giving the outside world a chance to intrude. Another part of him wanted to slide a ring on her left hand and show her off to all his friends.

"Am I holding us up again?" she asked, her voice sexy-husky with sleep.

"Nope. I figure with Patti not due home for a few more days, there's no hurry. We can eat Marthe's leftovers for breakfast, then leisurely pack up and get the babies."

She pouted.

"What's wrong?" he asked, tracing her down-turned lips.

"I was hoping for a repeat performance."

"Already?"

"Not up to the challenge?"

He laughed. "Them's fightin' words. Prepare to be dazzled."

DAZZLED? Lounging in bed, waiting for Jed to deliver her breakfast, Annie decided that what they'd just experienced was more in the realm of miracles.

She stretched and yawned, utterly content and as pleased with her cozy knotty-pine surroundings as she was with her companion.

They'd been without the babies for a whole night and morning, and look how well they were getting along. All her doubts about him not liking her for *her* were just silly insecurities. Leftover baggage from Conner that she needed to get rid of. As for her failed marriage to Troy, never had she been more determined to banish that disaster from her mind.

This was a morning for fresh starts.

"Hungry?" Jed asked. He carried a meagerly filled plate of leftover ribs and potato salad.

The sweet scent of Marthe's barbecue sauce made her stomach growl.

"Guess so," he said with a lazy smile while Annie put her hands over her noisy belly.

"Excuse me," she said. "I'm hungrier than I thought."

"What time do you usually eat breakfast?" he asked, setting the plate at the foot of the bed, then helping her sit up, bunching pillows behind her back.

"Six. I hardly ever sleep this late."

"Yeah. Me, neither."

"What do you eat?"

"You mean like am I a cereal or oatmeal kind of guy?"

"Right," she said as he set the plate on her lap, helping himself to a plump rib.

"I like bagels and cream cheese," she said. "Scrambled eggs, too. But believe me—" she said, grabbing a rib "—these work just fine."

"Good. Well, I'll leave you in peace to finish up."

Stay.

She wanted to say the word, but how could she when he was evidently eager to make his escape? Still, she had to say *something*. "Don't you want more to eat? I mean, there's not much, but we can share."

He shook his head. "I'm fine. Really, you take your time, and I'll start packing."

So this was it?

Fate's little kick in the pants to remind her not to get too comfortable?

Suddenly no longer hungry, Annie looked at her plate and wanted to cry.

After last night…

This morning…

Jed had been such a perfect lover. He satisfied her every need and deeper desires she hadn't even known she'd felt. How could she have misread him so badly? How could she have ignored all the warning signs that'd raged through her mind?

Her conscience laughed. *How could you have been so stupid? Do the names* Conner and Troy *ring any bells?*

Jed was nothing like them, but that didn't mean they'd make a perfect couple. Or that being with him was a magic ticket to happiness.

If anything, it could be just the opposite.

Chapter Twelve

Jed slammed the cupboard door above the sink.

Dammit.

What was wrong with him?

Why wasn't he in that bedroom right now, sharing ribs and more kisses with the woman of his dreams?

Because he wasn't good enough for her.

God, look at the way he'd rambled on in there about stupid stuff like what she ate for breakfast.

What could he offer a woman like Annie?

A lifetime of dealing with his neuroses?

Ah, now those he had plenty of. Searching for his sister had turned into a total disaster. If he'd just stayed calm the way he did at work, instead of getting all freaked-out, they wouldn't have made this trip.

And then what?

He would never have gotten to know Annie beyond neighborly waves across the breezeway.

Frowning, Jed worked double-time packing the rest of their stuff.

Maybe never knowing Annie would've been best....

"SURE YOU'VE GOT everything?" Jed asked, glancing at Annie. He climbed behind the wheel of Marthe's red Jeep, then pulled his door shut.

No, Annie wasn't at all sure she had everything.

In fact, she was pretty certain her heart was being left behind.

"Do you think there's something still inside?" Jed asked when she'd settled onto the seat beside him but hadn't closed her door.

She swallowed the knot in her throat.

Yes. She'd left the feel of his kisses and his hand-holding and touching her breasts. The feel of him being so deep inside her she'd forgotten where she ended and he began.

"Nope," she said, closing her door, then wiping tears from her cheeks so she could face him with a bright smile. "I'm all set to hit the road."

To get back to her safe, quiet condo where no paint would charm its way into her life only to leave her embarrassed, confused and alone.

"Great." He clapped his hands and rubbed them together. Did he have any idea how his eagerness to leave shattered the beauty of everything they'd shared? "Let's go."

Sure, let's go… So they could be that much closer to home, where she'd once again nurse her bleeding emotional wounds. Alone…

"SO?" MARTHE ASKED with a big wink. She held a steaming coffee mug in her left hand and nudged Annie with her right elbow. "Did all that by-yourselves time ignite any sparks?"

"What sparks?" Annie asked, hoping her new friend would drop the subject. She scooped Pia from a high chair. The baby smelled like her pink lotion and the sugar-sweetened rice cereal Marthe and Kayla had fed the triplets for breakfast.

"Oh, come on. You two couldn't wait to get us out of there. Well? Did Jed kiss you? Did more happen? Come on, girl, spill it."

"Sorry." Annie kissed the crown of Pia's downy head. "We just spent a quiet night playing Scrabble."

"Don't you believe her," Jed said, entering the dining room from the kitchen to casually rest his hands on her shoulders. "There was nothing quiet about the way she beat me."

Why was he doing this?

Pretending everything was great between them when nothing could be further from the truth?

Marthe said, "She ought to play King Murray over in Leadville. As far as I know, no one's ever beat him. Why don't you two take a day trip over there? Kayla and I will watch the babies. King's been off his feet for a few months now. He loves getting company."

"Who's King?" Annie asked, thrilled to have the topic off Jed and herself.

"Cantankerous old miner," Ditch said, doughnut to his mouth. He strolled in from the kitchen through the same door Jed had. "Old guy'll outlive us all. There's no real hurry to get back," he said. "How about it? You can take Marthe's Jeep. Head over Mosquito Pass. On a weekday, there should be hardly any traffic."

"What do you think?" Jed asked Annie.

Spending more time alone with him in this idyllic mountain setting—even one more day—was out of the question. Her spirit couldn't take it, knowing that their ultimate breakup was coming as soon as they got home.

Wishing she could shout her true feelings, she simply shrugged. "Sounds like a good time, but we probably ought to just head home. I've got to get my classroom ready and I still haven't completely unpacked at my condo."

"You're right," Jed agreed, crushing Annie when he didn't try to change her mind. "I need to get back to work, too."

"Aw, you guys are no fun." Marthe held out her arms. "At least give me a few more minutes with this cutie."

Annie handed Pia over.

Ditch said, "Come on, then, let's check your oil and tires. When Zane installed your new battery, he said you'd been burning oil."

Jed shook his head. "Patti and Howie bought the van used, but it's only three years old. I can't believe—" He'd been about to rag on his sister and brother-in-law for not taking better care of their vehicle, but stopped himself. No more. As Annie had said the night before, it was time to let his sister go.

She was a grown woman. If she didn't care that her van burned oil, neither should he.

See? He was slowly but surely getting a handle on this control thing.

"Ready?" Jed asked Annie, wishing she'd taken Marthe and Ditch up on their offer to watch the triplets just one more day. Her decision was the right one, but that didn't make her apparent rejection of him any easier to bear.

While Annie and Marthe checked the house for stray baby items, Jed shook Ditch's hand and thanked him for all his help.

"Forget it," Ditch said. "I didn't do anything you wouldn't have done for me." He leaned in closer to Jed. "Marthe's gonna kill me if I don't get the inside scoop. Did you and Annie, uh, hook up last night?"

Jed made a face. "Jeez, Ditch, has anyone ever told you that your social skills are sadly lacking?"

His old friend rolled his eyes. "I'll take that as your wounded male pride telling me not only didn't you get any, but your odds for the future aren't looking too good, either. Too bad…" He made a clucking sound. "The two of you are cute together. Annie and Marthe seemed to hit it off, too. I was hoping maybe we'd get to see more of you."

"Oh, you'll probably be seeing plenty of me, just not Annie."

"Ouch." Ditch winced. "Didn't even make it to first base?"

Jed slapped his friend on his back. "Buddy, I didn't even make it on the field."

NEARLY A HUNDRED MILES from the cabin where she'd allowed herself to fall for an amazing guy who only wanted her for her babysitting skills, Annie slipped off her sandals and propped her feet on the dash.

The heat radiating from the van's windows grew uncomfortable.

Just like the silence between her and Jed.

"The babies seem to be riding better," he said in the tunnel through Loveland Pass.

"It's probably the cereal Marthe fed them for breakfast. Solid foods sometimes help infants sleep."

"Oh." Outside the tunnel, he turned off the van's lights. "How come Patti hasn't been trying that?"

"She might have, which would explain why they were so put out with us. They wanted a more substantial meal than formula."

"Oh."

That's all you can say? Oh?

Annie gritted her teeth.

How could he stand the tension? That morning, they'd been in each other's arms, and now, they talked less than when they were strangers.

Had their night together been nothing to him but a quick roll in the hay?

Jed veered the van onto the side of the highway, and parked on the wide shoulder. "Out with it."

"Out with what?" she asked, traffic whizzing by. A monstrous tractor trailer made the small van shudder. "Is this safe?"

"I'll tell you what isn't—this brick wall you've been making me bust through all morning. If I ticked you off about something, tell me. Don't just sit here glowering the whole ride home."

She crossed her arms. "I'm not glowering."

"The hell you aren't. Look, I'm a big boy. Now that you've had a few hours to think about it, if last night and this morning were a mistake to you, I can take it. Just tell me. We'll agree to keep things casual once we get home."

"Oh, you're a big boy, all right. Big enough to give me what was obviously nothing more than a *thank-you* lay for my babysitting services?"

He flinched. "Please tell me you didn't just say what I think you did, because—"

From the back seat came a whimper. Judging by the low-pitched sound, it was Ronnie. Annie glanced over her shoulder and, sure enough, it was him. She jiggled his carrier, then got a teething ring from the diaper bag.

"Annie? I'm still waiting for an answer."

"Just stop it, Jed. As you've so graciously pointed out, we're both adults here. I don't know what I expected from you—if anything, maybe that you'd at least sit and have leftovers with me. But *nooooo,* you were in such an all-fired hurry to get away, you couldn't even stand to share a meal, let alone a conversation more meaningful than what we eat for breakfast."

He dropped his head back. "You've got to be kidding. That's what you're upset about? The fact that I didn't eat breakfast with you?"

"You wouldn't have found it a little upsetting if the tables had been turned?"

"Okay…" He reached for Annie's hand and gave it a squeeze. She wanted to snatch it back to the safety of her lap, but physically, emotionally, she couldn't. Just this simple touch meant so much. "First off," he said, "you can't imagine how badly I wanted to stay in that bed and share leftovers with you. But the problem was, if I had eaten that food, there wouldn't have been any for you."

"You mean that's all there was?"

"That's what I just said, isn't it?"

"But there were plenty of ribs left over last night."

"Three a.m. snacks?"

"Oh." Now *Annie* was the one with no comment. How had he done it? The creep. Now she felt bad for scraping her meal into the trash.

"I was trying to be a good guy by leaving you to your feast. And that's why I now have raging heartburn from the dozen doughnuts I put away at Marthe and Ditch's."

"And that's my fault?"

"Heck, yeah."

Despite herself, she grinned, although she was far

from convinced that altruism was the full reason he'd left her alone in the bed.

"Look at me," she said.

"Why?" He looked out his side window at a passing red car, instead.

"Because, after all we've shared, I think you owe me that much."

Since he didn't turn away from the window, he obviously didn't agree.

"All right, then," she said with a deep sigh. "You can do it without looking me in the eyes."

"Do what?"

"Tell me your supposed fear of my impending starvation was the only reason you left me alone in that room."

"God, woman." He slammed his palm against the steering wheel. "What do you want from me?"

"The truth." Every bone in her body urged her to jump out of the van and run when Jed had hit the steering wheel, but she stood her ground.

She was no longer a scared newlywed.

He wasn't Troy.

When Jed finally looked at Annie, her gaze was solidly on him. The instant their eyes met, she knew she was on the right track. The man was definitely lying. And if they had to sit here on the side of the road until Christmas, she intended to find out what he was lying about.

"Oh, hell," he eventually said. "You're not going to let this go, are you?"

She shook her head.

"Okay, then, the truth is that you looked so damned beautiful…lying there with your hair all messed up and nothing on but my ratty old sheets. I felt I should've given you more. That I should *be* more."

"You're kidding, right?"

"Do I look like it?"

Judging by his down-turned brows and lips—no. Jed still held her hand, and she tightly gripped his.

Annie asked, "Don't you have a clue how much I've come to care for you?" She shook her head again, glancing out the window while swallowing new tears. "I mean, when I first met you with all those crying babies in your arms, I was captivated. But then the more I saw you in action…going off to work, where you save the world one house, one family, at a time. And then how you tried to save your sister… You're a special breed of man."

Releasing her to cover his face with both hands, Jed said, "I should've just kidnapped you today. Taken you over to Mosquito Pass to give you the pleasure of letting my friend, King, soundly whomp your sweet little butt."

"I would've liked that," she said.

"Then why didn't you say so?"

"Because I thought you didn't want to."

He groaned.

"What's wrong now?" Annie asked.

"It's a good two hours back to the cabin. By the time

we get to Marthe and Ditch's to drop off the babies, it's too late to get out there today."

"True. But as Ditch pointed out, now that we know Patti's okay, and she's not due home with Howie for another couple of days, there's really no rush."

Except that every second she was with him, she fell a little more in love.

Annie suddenly had a tough time finding her next breath. *Love?* Was that what made her stomach hurt and feel wonderful at the same time? They'd weathered their first fight and Jed had been the one to start the healing. What kind of man did that?

A very special man, just as she'd told him.

A keeper.

He put the van back in gear and did a U-turn at the next exit.

Annie's pulse hammered a little more quickly.

Granted, Jed's words had been ultrasweet, but that didn't mean he was ready for marriage. Neither was she. She'd just recovered from a crushing blow with Conner, and before that, a disastrous marriage to Troy.

Those things pretty much guaranteed it wasn't love she was feeling, but a giddy, strange mixture of emotions ranging from relief—because this trip had taken her mind off her more pertinent troubles—to a physical yearning for more of Jed's kisses.

Yes, she should've told Jed that the idea of going to meet this King person was nice but that she really ought to head home.

She had things to do.

A bathroom that needed painting.

So why did absolutely nothing in the world sound more appealing than driving over a mountain to play Scrabble with a man who might very well beat her as badly as her grandmother did?

Why? Because all of that would happen with Jed by her side.

Chapter Thirteen

"Aaarrgghhh!" Annie cried. "Slow down. We're going to crash!"

Jed laughed. "You need to relax. I've done this a hundred times. Trust me, we'll be fine." She stopped screeching, but still had a white-knuckled grip on the support handle built into the dash.

On this stretch of road before the summit, the ruts in the dirt road were particularly deep—in some places, three or four feet. Jed would never tell Annie, but the drive was proving to be more challenging than he'd expected. But that was okay, because once the day's diversion was over, he'd have another night alone with Annie back at the cabin.

"Do you see how far down it is over there?"

He glanced in the direction Annie pointed. "That's nothing. I've been on old mining trails up the sides of sheer cliffs."

"Yeah, well, maybe I'd be better off back at the outlet mall."

"You didn't have enough of that yesterday?" They'd stopped off on the way back to the cabin. Jed had told Annie that he wanted to get the babies out of the car for a while, but he'd really stopped for her. Jeez, their first time through, she'd looked at the place like a dog catching sight of a bone—only it wasn't bones she was after, but bargain-priced clothes and purses.

He'd lost count of the hours he'd spent sitting outside dressing rooms jiggling the babies in their stroller. But looking at the hot little denim miniskirt and tight pale-blue T-shirt she had on today, Jed had to admit that every one of those hours had been worth it.

"A woman can never get enough shopping. Remember that, and any woman will adore you forever."

What if I don't want any woman, just you?

He shook his head lightly. The altitude must be affecting his reason. They'd gotten along better than ever since their talk, but they still had some incredibly large barriers between them—his pigheaded need to be in control.

Who knew where the next few days would lead? And when they returned home, she'd probably be asked on a ton of dates by rich single dads who could afford the steep tuition at the private preschool where she worked.

They'd be professional men who never came home reeking of smoke, even after a shower.

Guys who didn't work twenty-four-hour shifts and didn't have soot under their nails.

"You're awfully quiet over there," Annie said. "Is that a sign that this road is in worse shape than you've been letting on?"

"Nope." But *he* was in worse shape. Why couldn't he just live in the moment and let the future sort itself out? Lots of women liked firemen. Why should Annie be any different?

Because she was.

Different from most women—*better*—in every conceivable way.

"Are we almost to the top?"

"Yep. And from up there, the view is going to make this bumpy ride worth it."

"Promise?"

"Absolutely."

"All right, then, I'll try to relax. But between worrying that we're about to slide off the mountain and wondering just how badly I'm going to be beaten at Scrabble, I have to say that this hasn't been the most peaceful of days."

"It's not supposed to be peaceful, remember? This is my revenge for the way you crushed me again last night." He'd started the game in the lead, but then he'd caught a whiff of the end-of-the-day scent that was all Annie. A little sweat, a little baby lotion, a whole lot of temptation to resist.

"Hey—it's not my fault you kept drawing bad letters."

Right. No more than it'd been his fault that he'd kept getting distracting peeks down her shirt. Had it really been less than twenty-four hours since he'd tasted what now he could only dream of?

"Yeah, well, you just wait," he said. "King's going to beat you so bad you'll cry—not that I'm looking forward to that part."

"You're mean," she said, sticking out her tongue.

"Check out that view, then tell me I'm mean."

He floored it to get the Jeep over the last big rise, then they'd arrived.

For as far as the eye could see, green forests accentuated the snowcapped peaks. Jed had climbed many of the mountains in the area. Others he'd four-wheeled. But none of those adventures meant as much as being here with Annie.

He parked the Jeep next to the wooden sign serving as a memorial to Father Dyer, a man who'd brought not only religion to the mining town of Leadville in the late 1800s, but mail.

Openmouthed, Annie climbed out and slipped on a light denim jacket. Hand to her forehead, she shaded her eyes from the sun. "Oh, Jed, it's amazing. I feel like we're alone on top of the world."

At this time of day, on a weekend, the spot would be covered with sightseers, but on a Wednesday, Annie and Jed had it all to themselves.

He wanted to lace his fingers with hers and draw her into a kiss, but things were almost comfortable between them again. Why risk doing anything that might harm their fragile new bond?

As good as their relationship currently felt, he couldn't help wondering if they'd somehow gotten it backward by sleeping together so soon. Their making love had been great, but at the same time, it was probably a mistake.

Did Annie feel the same way? Was that part of the underlying tension between them?

Jed had never been the type to casually sleep around. Making love implied a certain level of commitment. He and Annie were practically strangers, yet on a soul-deep level, he'd never felt closer to a woman.

"Thank you for bringing me here," she said.

"Thanks for coming."

"Are you okay?" she asked, nudging his arm.

"Sure. Why? Do I look sick?"

"No. You're just awfully quiet. In fact, you've been quiet ever since I thought we patched things up."

A gust of wind took her OU ball cap.

She shrieked and laughed as she tried to catch it, but the wind sent it skittering across the rocks.

Jed chased it down, then perched it back on her curls. "I forgot to tell you back at the cabin, but you look cute in that."

"Thanks."

"You're welcome."

"Well?" she asked, not looking at the view but at him. "Are you going to tell me what's bothering you?"

"For starters—" he tugged on the bill of her cap "—I

bring you all the way up here and all you want to do is analyze me."

"I'm not analyzing you, Jed. I'm showing an interest in your thoughts and feelings. There's a difference, you know." Her kissable lips frowned.

Jed frowned right back. All the signs were there—he was in deep trouble.

"Are you ticked that I ate the last doughnut for breakfast?"

He rolled his eyes.

"Did I snore or hog the covers?"

"What's the matter with you? Why do you have to keep harping at me when we're in this beautiful setting?" *Why can't you just step into my arms and let me hold you while we take in the view?*

"I'm not harping."

"Then what do you call it?"

Annie looked away from him to hide her irrational tears.

What she called it was frustration!

Honestly, how many hints did she have to give the guy before he'd hold her hand or kiss her? Ever since they'd made love, it was as if he'd adopted a hands-off policy, and it was driving her completely nuts.

"Why won't you kiss me?" she finally blurted.

"W-what?"

"You heard me."

"Okay, I haven't kissed you because I thought we weren't going to do that anymore."

"Says who?" She stubbornly raised her chin.

"Me." Jed turned his back on her, mounting a steep dirt trail.

"Oh, so Mr. Control has the final say on everything—including matters of the heart?" Annie chased after him, one hand on her hat, the other holding the flapping halves of her open jacket.

"I didn't hear mention of any hearts." He kept right on walking.

She kept right on chasing. "Yeah, well, if you'd been listening, you'd know I didn't imply any specific hearts, just the general premise."

He stopped and turned to face her. "And if *you'd* been listening, you'd see that I want to kiss you—a lot. But I'm no fool, Annie. Your body language says it loud and clear—hands off."

She laughed. "Really?"

"Yes, really."

"Sorry to bust your ego there, fella, but you might want a refresher course in Body Language One-Oh-One, because ever since you were so honest with me yesterday—not to mention your patience at all of those outlet malls—I've thought of nothing but doing this…"

On tiptoe, Annie seized initial control of their kiss, but then Jed swept his strong fingers under the fall of her hair, cupping her head, tilting it to get their lips at a better angle. He urged her mouth open, caressing her tongue with his. Waves of hunger and need shimmered through her.

She crept her hands up under his T-shirt, gliding her fingertips along the warm, smooth skin of his back.

"Woman," he said on the heels of a groan. "You make me crazy."

"Ditto," she said before he started to kiss her all over again.

Next intermission, he asked, "Why are we always fighting when this is so much more fun?"

"New pact," she said.

"Let's hear it."

"Kiss first. Bicker later."

"Why do we have to bicker at all?"

"Good question. Let's kiss some more. Maybe that'll help us figure it out."

"YOU'RE LATE," King Murray said the instant he jerked open his door. He sat in an antique wicker wheelchair with a red flannel blanket across his lap. His white hair, beard and bushy eyebrows would have made him look like a cross between Santa and Colonel Sanders—but King didn't sport the requisite smile. "And from the whisker burn around that poor girl's lips, you should've shaved before mugging her in broad daylight."

"Nice to see you, too." Jed gave his old eccentric friend a hug and made formal introductions before asking, "How do you know I kissed Annie today and not last night?" He slipped his hand reassuringly around her waist.

"What kind of fool do you take me for?" King

slammed the door to his sweltering tin shack. He clicked five dead bolts into place. Great. Nothing like spending an afternoon locked in a sauna that reeked of wet newspapers and pipe tobacco. The guy could afford better, but he'd get all cantankerous when pressed to make improvements to his abode. He said he liked it just the way it was. Jed figured who was he to tell the old coot any different?

Jed smiled. "Expecting silver bandits?"

"You can never be too safe," the old man said, jerking his head toward the curtained-off entrance to his mine. "Doc says I'll be out of this chair soon. Come October, I aim to have a whole new shaft open. Once news hits town of the vein I'm gonna find, folks'll be linin' up to be my new best friend."

"Yeah, well, until then, how about a game of Scrabble?"

King snorted. "I've already beat you five ways to Sunday. What's the matter, need a little more stomping on your pride?"

Jed rubbed his palms together. "You're playing Annie, not me."

The old man roared with raspy laughter. "Me play that stick with curls? Not worth my time. Go on, both of you get lost. I've got plannin' to do on where to sink my next shaft."

"Not so fast there, Mr. Murray." Still ticked by his whisker-burn comment, Annie reached into her purse, grabbed her wallet, then slapped a twenty onto the nearest table. "Care to take me up on a friendly wager?" While the old man gawked at the money, Annie winked at Jed, who seemed equally surprised to find a pre-school teacher placing bets.

King cleared his throat. "Take a seat at the kitchen table. I'll get the board. Oh—do you like polka?"

FOUR HOURS and four Scrabble games later, Annie was up by eighty bucks—despite the accordions blaring from hidden stereo speakers. While King took a bath-room break, she whispered to Jed, "I feel awful taking his money. Is he on a fixed income?"

Jed chuckled. "The old coot's a millionaire ten times over. He was a Wall Street bigwig before he took up mining."

"For real?"

"Have you had a good look at the mantel?"

Annie looked in that direction and saw what she'd assumed was a Van Gogh print. "No way," she said, marching over for a better look. Up close, the painting's colors glowed.

"He's got a Monet over the john," Jed said. "I don't know if you noticed while answering my phone, but that Gauguin over my bed is the real deal. Marthe and King had this big art discussion one day, and she men-tioned I liked that painting. My next birthday, it came to my place via FedEx. Marthe said he bought it from some museum. Off part of the mine is a wine cellar where he stores vintage champagne. Come New

Year's, he's a real popular guy. Throws one great party."

"Sounds like fun," Annie said. "I'd love to go if—well, you know what I mean." She tucked her hands in her pockets for the short walk back to the table.

"If we're still together?" Jed asked.

She shrugged.

"Do you want to be?"

"How should I know?" she said, playing it cool despite her racing pulse and the knot in her stomach that felt as if she'd driven her car down a steep hill at sixty miles per hour. "We're practically strangers."

He took a step toward Annie, blasting her with his charming grin. "We didn't feel like strangers the other night."

With him so close, so handsome, so charming, so flirty and fun, she wasn't sure how to reply. Luckily, she didn't have to.

King rolled back into the room. "One more game, Curl Girl. Double or nothing. What do you say?"

From what she'd learned about the guy, Annie suspected he might be setting her up. One-hundred-and-sixty bucks bought a lot of paint. "I don't know," she said. "That's a great deal of money."

"Chicken?"

"No, but come on—I'm a preschool teacher. My job's rewarding, but not exactly lucrative."

He grunted, then wheeled over to a cheap metal filing cabinet and pulled open the creaky bottom drawer.

He fished something out, shut the drawer, then wheeled back. "How about this to sweeten the pot?" From out of a velvet pouch he withdrew a bejeweled egg.

Faberge?

She gulped. "Is that what I think it is?"

"Bah." He waved his hand in dismissal. "Got three more stashed around here somewhere. Wife liked 'em real well."

"Did she die?"

Jed coughed. "I've heard the Broncos are going to have a great season."

King glared at Annie. "The no-good wench said I spent too much time underground and not enough with her. She left me. Married some fool nightclub singer down in Phoenix." To Jed, he muttered, "If you ever tell anyone I said this, I'll flat out deny it, but son, once you two hitch up, make sure you don't spend too much time on the job. Work enough to pay the bills, but remember—you've got to tend your flowers."

"My *flowers,* huh?" Jed shot a wink Annie's way. "Does that mean I get more than one?"

BACK AT THE CABIN, over a dinner of deli sandwiches, chips and giant dill pickles, Annie eyed her Faberge egg. "I still can't believe he just gave this to me. The thing's got to be worth a fortune."

Jed shrugged. "It's only money. King was crazy for his wife, he just didn't always show it. She was a blonde. I suspect you remind him of her, otherwise he'd have whomped you five out of five games instead of letting you win."

"Oh—you think he *let* me win?"

"That's what I said, isn't it?" He dabbed the corners of his smile with a yellow paper napkin. "Because what Marthe and I failed to tell you, is that while you're good, he's *nationally ranked* good."

"So the whole day was a setup?"

"It was supposed to be," he said, before taking a bite of ham sandwich. "Who could've guessed King would actually take a liking to you? He hates everyone."

Reaching across the table, Jed laced his fingers with Annie's. "You wanna be in my garden? I'm going to take old King's advice and tend my flowers well." He waggled his eyebrows.

"Beast."

"Your beast if you'll have me."

"Yeah, but for how long?" she whispered, shocked that she'd asked the question, dizzy from the pace of her heart.

"How long do you want?"

"You're talking in circles."

"So are you." He raised her hand to his lips.

Closing her eyes, Annie willed her pulse to slow. How many sides did the man have? Here was yet another. A soft, romantically teasing side that she adored every bit as much as his many others.

"Do you think you could stand being mine for a month?"

Unable to speak, she nodded.

"How about two?"

She nodded again.

"Want to be my date for King's New Year's party? We could head out right after Christmas. Ski Copper Mountain and Breckenridge, then—" He stopped himself. "Listen to me. Taking over your holidays when I know you've got family obligations."

"Yes. My grandmother."

"So you probably don't want to do anything for New Year's?"

She wrinkled her nose. "I'm thinking we might want to work on our communication skills."

"That's a given, but you still haven't told me if you're penciling me in for the holidays."

Slipping her arms around his neck, she pressed her lips to his, telling him in the plainest way she knew…

Yes—to skiing and New Year's and most anything else he might want to offer.

Chapter Fourteen

There, beside the small oak table where their meals sat, half-eaten, Jed drew Annie to her feet, sliding his hands to the small of her back, deepening their kiss with bold strokes of his tongue.

"I'm not even sure how it happened," he said, "but I love you, Annie Harnesberry. We've both had some tough times, but somehow this—*us*—feels right."

Her cheek against his chest, she nodded, surrendering herself to the feel of his heartbeat, so steady and sure.

Yes, a tiny voice inside still warned her to be careful—not to jump into something she wasn't ready for. But then the voice of reason kicked in, reminding her that Jed was nothing like either of the men who'd hurt her so badly before.

Like Troy, Jed wanted to be in control, but he proved every day that he didn't *have* to be. He never hit when he didn't get his way. He didn't even yell.

And when she'd asked Jed if he only wanted her

around as a sitter for his niece and nephews, his answer was all she could ever hope for and more.

So as she watched him unfasten the buttons of her denim jacket, did she feel ready to make an unofficial commitment to Jed even though she barely knew him?

Yes, because she *did* know him.

In her soul.

Where it truly counted.

He eased her jacket off her shoulders and arms, draping it over the back of her chair.

She shivered, and he ran his large, warm hands up and down her shoulders. "Cold?"

"Uh-huh."

"Nervous?"

"How did you know?"

"Your lower lip quivers."

"It does?"

He nodded, outlining her mouth with the tip of his index finger. "And your pupils widen."

"Sorry," she wasn't sure what else to say.

"I don't want you to be sorry," he said. "I love that about you. That I know what you're thinking."

I love that about you, too.

"Do you want to know what *I'm* thinking?" he asked.

She nodded, and he skimmed his finger lower, down her chin and throat. Making a sharp right at her collarbone, he etched a new path under her thin cotton T-shirt to the strap of her bra. Slipping his finger underneath, he said, "With your consent, I'd like to take you to bed, then just hold you all night long. Does that sound okay?"

"More than okay… Perfect."

NEVER HAD ANNIE awakened happier or more content, as if all was right with her world.

Jed lay on his back beside her, broad chest bare. His hair was always spiked and messy, but this morning especially so. Was he one of those who moved around a lot in their sleep? She'd slept so soundly beside him, she didn't have a clue.

She curved her hand over his shoulder, grinning when it didn't reach even halfway around.

At the time she'd left him, Troy's size had frightened her. Jed's size had always made her feel more secure.

She closed her eyes and sighed, reflecting on how much her life had changed in less than a week's time.

In a roundabout way, Jed had proposed, and she'd accepted.

"What's got you so deep in thought?" he asked, startling her.

Hand to her chest, she said, "Jeez. You scared me to death."

"Sorry." He drew her into his arms. After kissing her forehead, he moved on to her lips.

"Mmm…you're forgiven."

"Thanks." After a few minutes of holding her, he asked, "Hungry?"

"Not really. You?"

He shook his head. "I'm actually not feeling so hot."

"You don't think you're coming down with something, do you?"

"Nah. Just nerves."

She scooted up in the bed to see his face better. "About what?" *Not us, I hope.*

"There goes that quivering lip of yours," he said with the slow, sexy grin she'd come to love. "Trust me, this has nothing to do with you, okay? I'm wondering what I'm going to say when I see Patti."

"What do you mean? Won't you simply be happy to see her?"

Bunching a pillow under his head, he shrugged. "Of course, I'll be glad she's home safe, but it's more complicated than that."

"How so?"

"It just is. But it shouldn't be, so I'll shut up."

"You don't have to on my account. Go ahead, explain how you feel."

"That's the thing," he said, drawing her against him, playing with one of her curls. "I don't even know myself—except when it comes to how I feel about you."

"Which is?" she teased.

"Good." He kissed the crown of her head. "Very, very good."

"I'M GOING to miss you," Marthe said, practically suffocating Jed with the strength of her hug. Ditch helped Annie gather and load the last of the baby gear.

"You've hardly seen me," he said, hugging Marthe back.

"I know, but somehow just having you here feels like old times. Like back when we were kids, hanging out all summer. No responsibilities, just fun." She swiped at a few fat tears.

"Hey," he said, "I already told you Annie and I will be back for New Year's. She wants to fix her grandmother up with King."

Laughing through her tears, Marthe said, "Annie told me. I think it's a super idea."

"So why are you still crying?"

"Oh, God, Jed. I'm pregnant. I've suspected it for a while, but I just took one of those home tests this morning. Ditch doesn't know yet."

"Why the tears?" Jed asked. "He's going to be thrilled."

"No," she said. "We can barely afford the two we have." With Sponge Bob blaring on TV, she cried all the harder, leaving Jed not sure what to do. Of course, he held on to her for dear life, but what could he say? The financial aspect of having kids was a sobering fact.

While he couldn't be more pleased about how things were going with Annie, he'd made love to her twice without protection. She could be pregnant. Sure, he had savings—more than enough to feel comfortable asking Annie to marry him, *if* and *when* it came to that point. But he didn't have nearly enough to raise and support a baby—or babies—of their own.

But if Annie told him on the drive back to Pecan that she was expecting his son or daughter, he'd be thrilled despite any financial hardships they'd encounter. And so would his good friend Ditch when he heard the news about the latest addition to his own family.

After telling Marthe just that, Jed said, "Do you want me to break it to him for you?"

She sniffled and shook her head. "I think I'll farm Kayla and Billy out to Ditch's mom this weekend, then let him know over a steak and baked potato—plenty of butter. He's always in a good mood after eating butter."

"Aren't we all?" Jed said with a laugh.

"I think we're ready." Annie stepped up behind Jed, slipping her arms around his waist. "Mmm...I missed you."

Marthe cast Jed her first real smile since they'd arrived. "I can't wait to make Ditch pay up on that thirty-minute massage he owes me for losing our bet."

Easing beside Jed, Annie said, "I still can't believe you two bet on whether or not Jed and I would—Marthe? What's wrong? You look like you've been crying."

"Wh-where's Ditch?" she managed to ask.

"Outside with the kids," Annie said. "Billy got gum on one of the front stroller wheels, so Ditch is making him scrape it off."

"He's such a g-good father," Marthe said, starting to cry all over again.

Annie was instantly by her side, putting her arm

around her friend's slumped shoulders. "Please tell me what's wrong."

Marthe did.

And when she'd finished, Annie snatched a paper towel from the counter and wiped her cheeks. "I think this is fabulous. You two are great with kids. Why shouldn't you have more?"

"B-because they cost a fortune. There are medical bills and clothes and lessons and college and—"

Annie said, "Wait here. I've got just the thing to ease your mind."

Annie left the room and returned with a black velvet pouch in hand. "Once we're gone, I want you to open this. It's yours."

Marthe's eyes widened as she accepted the gift. "It's heavy. What is it?"

"Your first baby gift from me to you. Now, stop worrying and start celebrating. Babies are supposed to bring joy." Annie kissed her friend's forehead, then told her how much she'd miss her with a heartfelt hug.

THEY'D SAID their goodbyes, loaded up the babies and were on their way home, but even fifty miles down the road, Jed couldn't believe what Annie had done for Marthe and Ditch.

He finally asked, "Do you have any idea how much that egg must be worth?"

"I'm hoping it's enough to buy a truckload of diapers and several years college tuition."

"I'd say it's worth a damn sight more than that. What made you give it away?"

Annie lifted those adorable feet of hers onto the dash and wriggled her toes. "A pretty selfish reason actually."

"Okay, let's hear it."

With a smile, she asked, "Why should I tell you?"

"Because after all we've been through, we're a team. And that's pretty much a rule in all team sports—no secrets kept from other team members."

"Oh, well, in that case…" The cocky look she gave him made him want to pinch one of her pink-tipped toes.

"I'm waiting," he said, slowing to take the next curve on the winding road lined with ponderosa pines and stands of aspen.

"With us so happy, I couldn't stand seeing Marthe so sad. I figured, what the heck? It wasn't as if I'd even had time to become attached to the egg. And anyway, I figure King would approve of my decision."

"I figure you're right. So? What did you think about Marthe being so upset about her pregnancy?"

"I can't say I blame her. Finances are something to consider."

"Yeah, I thought so, too."

"Plus, there's the whole age issue. Kayla and Billy are already half-raised. It's got to be scary thinking you have your child-rearing days almost behind you, and then starting over again."

"You do want kids, though, right?" The second the

question was out, Jed wished he hadn't asked. He'd broached the subject the other day when they'd been fooling around, but this time he was serious. What if Annie said no?

"Absolutely."

His shoulders slumped with relief. Good. He wanted kids, too. Maybe not today, but soon.

"You?"

When he nodded, her expression brightened.

And together, babies for once contentedly napping, Annie and Jed rode out the miles that brought them closer to their futures.

"YOU'RE NOT PREGNANT, are you?" Jed asked just past the exit for the Denver International Airport.

"What?" Annie looked at him sharply, brushing away tears.

"You're crying. And it hasn't been that long since we heard Marthe's news."

Annie rolled her eyes. "No. I'm not pregnant—at least, I don't think so."

"So what's the matter?"

"Look in your mirror. The mountains are so beautiful. How can you stand to leave them?"

Jed laughed—not because he thought she was being silly, but because he understood how she felt. "Patti and my mom always cried when we left. Dad never knew if they were crying because our vacation was over, or because of their feelings about the mountains."

"Maybe a little of both," Annie said, blowing her nose on a fast-food napkin she'd found between the seats. "I didn't expect to have so much fun. This might sound a little odd, but since we're members of the same team…"

"Yeah, yeah," he said, eyes smiling.

"I know this trip was good for you in that it jolted you into realizing that Patti's capable of looking after herself. It was also good for me. The past few years haven't been all that great, and I was beginning to think I'd never trust again."

Jed reached across the space between them, and locked his fingers with hers. "Thanks. After what Patti put me through, you can't know how much that means to me. For a while there, I felt like I was going out of my mind."

"Patti might not know it, but she's very lucky to have you."

"Right about now, *I* feel like the lucky one."

From the back, one baby started to cry, then another and another.

Jed groaned. "I had to go and jinx us, didn't I?"

"Hey," Annie said, pointing to a run-down billboard in the shape of a giant sunflower. "Look on the bright side. We're only fifteen miles from the world's only working car made entirely from sunflower seeds—excluding the engine, of course."

"Oh, of course." Jed smiled.

"ANNIE, HONEY, wake up." Jed lightly shook her awake.

Hands prayered beneath her cheek, her legs drawn up in what appeared to be an uncomfortable position beneath her, she said, "Where are we? What time is it?"

"We're home. And it's about three in the afternoon." After getting a late start the previous morning, they'd taken their time, and even spent the night in a motel outside Salina.

Annie inched into an upright position so slowly, it made Jed cringe.

"What hurts?"

"Everything," she said. "Remind me not to fall asleep sideways again."

"Gotcha. But you were so out of it after that last diaper stop, I think you would've fallen asleep standing on your head." He grinned, smoothing his hand across her rumpled curls.

"So we're really home? As in Pecan?"

"Yep. I already put the babies inside. I just left the van running with the air on so you wouldn't bake. Compared to that perfect mountain weather, being in this heat again pretty much sucks."

"We could always go back."

"Believe me, if it weren't for the twenty or so messages from my captain, the second we get hold of Patti, that's exactly what I'd suggest we do."

"You're not in trouble, are you?"

"Nah. The boss just gets cranky in all this heat."

"But isn't he used to it? He's a fireman."

"Good point," he said. "The next time I feel like going on a suicide mission, I'll be sure to bring that up."

"HOW ARE YOU DOING?" Annie asked at about eight, rocking Pia in her arms.

Patti and Howie's plane had landed in Tulsa at six-forty, and they were due at Jed's apartment any minute.

Jed shrugged. "I'm all right. I'll be better once I've got you all to myself, though."

She laughed, relieved to see him able to joke about their situation. Truthfully, she'd been worried about how his meeting with Patti would go. The way he'd first talked about letting his sister have it had spooked her.

Before hitting her, Troy had yelled—loudly enough that the last time, the time he'd sent her to the hospital—the neighbors had called the police. If they hadn't, who knows where she'd be now? Or if she'd even be alive.

Truck lights shone through the slats of the mashed-potato-beige vertical blinds on Jed's windows. She made a face. "We've got to get you some color in here."

"What's wrong with my place?"

"Everything," she said. "Where should I start?"

A car door slammed shut

A few seconds later, another.

Annie watched helplessly as a muscle popped in Jed's jaw. What was he thinking? "Is there anything I can do to help?" she asked.

Hand possessively on her bare thigh, he said, "Don't leave me."

She nodded just as a knock sounded on the door. "Jed?" a woman's voice called out. "It's us."

Chapter Fifteen

Jed looked at Howie's crutches, bruised cheeks, black left eye and right foot in a cast. He knew that as awful as Howie looked nearly a week after the accident, he must've really been bad off when his sister left town to be with him. But an hour of watching Patti coo over her babies, acting as if nothing had ever happened, filled him with slow-burning frustration.

While Jed was in the kitchen getting everyone Cokes, playing along with Patti's *everything's normal* routine, he couldn't stop from replaying the desperation he'd felt. The sheer knife-edged panic that'd seized him the moment he'd realized something serious had happened to his sister.

He'd had the same feeling when his little brother was in the house dying. The same feeling when his parents had died and when Patti became a wild teen, running with the wrong crowd, determined to destroy her life before it'd even begun.

He looked up and Patti was in the kitchen. Grinning

up at him with her glass held under the ice dispenser on the fridge, she said, "Some excitement, huh? Aside from the fact that Howie was hurt and my ankle's sprained, I haven't had such an adventure since—"

"An *adventure?* You think this week was an adventure?"

She waved off his concern. "Good grief, Jed, stop being such an old grouch. You know what I mean. The adventure of it. All this flying and driving and trying to get in touch with each other. In retrospect, it's been quite exciting. Maybe we ought to do it all again, only—"

"Dammit, Patti!" Jed smacked his palm against a cabinet door. "This is so typical of you. Every grandma and her poodle has a cell phone these days, but—"

"Speaking of which, where was *your* cell while all of this was going on?"

Count on Patti to bring up his mistake when he was in the middle of bawling her out. Glaring at his feet, he said, "My phone was back here, but we're talking about you. About how you didn't reach me before I left for the cabin. You just left me here with three infants. *Me.* A bachelor who doesn't know the first thing about babies. And you just took off, without even trying to get word to me, what—"

"I did try! At least fifty times. Do you want me to list them all? One, at the airport, only you weren't home. Two, at—"

"Knock it off!" Jed raged, unable to keep his anger with her at bay.

In the living room, Annie jumped. The last time she'd heard yelling like that was with Troy.

Howie moaned. "Oh, no, here they go. Jed means well, but where Patti's concerned, he's never learned to let go."

"She's all he has."

"I know," Howie said. "It's the same for her with him. I mean, I know she has me now, too, but it's different with Jed. They have a strange bond that I'm still trying to figure out."

Jed railed on. "This has to be your last stunt, Patti. The last time you're going to act like a child. Running off without telling anyone where you were going was just that—childish. No matter what the circumstance. What if the babies had been older? Old enough to know that Mommy was gone, and worry that she might not be coming back? What could I have told them?"

"I'm sorry," Patti said, her voice broken. "I didn't *not* call you on purpose, Jed, any more than you purposely forgot your cell. You act like I deliberately set out to push your buttons. God, you always think the worst of me."

"I think I'll go referee," Howie said, reaching for his crutches.

Annie clasped her fingers tightly on her lap, glad the babies were upstairs sleeping.

"That's just it!" Jed roared. "You've done a crap-load of button-pushing in the past, Patti. Remember the time you called me wasted from Jasper Henning's party?

You asked me to come and get you, then you took off with Greg Davis. You didn't come home for three days. And how about the time you—"

"Shut up!" Patti fired back. "I'm not a messed-up kid any more."

"No," he said. "You're mother who thought nothing of hopping on a plane without—"

Annie squeezed her eyes shut.

What was she doing?

Jed's raised voice sounded remarkably like Troy's.

Her ex-husband yelled first, and hit later.

Was that how it would be with Jed? After all, if he yelled at his sister, what was to stop him from yelling at his girlfriend—or his wife?

Annie knew better than to have fallen for him. How many warning signs had she chosen to ignore? His controlling nature. His seeming perfection. And now the yelling.

It was all the same.

How blind was she? How dumb?

Had she learned nothing in the past five years? All along she'd been worried that Jed only liked her for her skills with the babies. Ha. That was nothing compared to the dark truth she was now finding out.

Troy had begun their relationship making Annie believe he was the answer to her every prayer. He'd bought her flowers and candy and sung her sappy love songs on karaoke night down at their favorite local bar.

Annie grabbed her purse, then crept out the front door.

"You dumb, bitch. I told you to get light beer. You know I'm in training for that bodybuilding show at the gym."

"I'm sorry, Troy. They were out of light. I figured this would do."

"Yeah, well you figured wrong." He slammed his fist against the wall, creating one more dent among many.

Cringing inside, always inside herself, Annie fussed with the dish towel that hung from the rack beside the sink.

So pretty.

She'd just focus on the pretty pink cabbage roses.

The towels had been a gift from her grandmother, who'd warned her about Troy. Grams told Annie she was marrying him too fast. That she was trying to escape the pain she felt over losing her grandfather, then her parents to another overseas assignment. Looking for shortcuts to achieve her dream of starting her own family.

Bam.

Instead of the wall, Troy turned to Annie, smacking her hard across the face. "The next time I tell you to get light, if State Line's out, go to another store. You know I had a bad day down at the plant. Why do you want to go and ruin my night, too?"

"I—I don't," she said, slipping further inside herself.

He hit her again. "Get the hell out of here. Don't come back until you've got the right beer."

Annie hadn't bothered coming back at all.

In the Emergency Room, she'd filed a police report. The next day, divorce papers. With no children, and practically no shared property, the matter was settled soon enough—especially since Troy already had his next female punching bag in line.

Annie tried to warn the girl, but it hadn't done any good. Charmed senseless by Troy's good looks and honed body, Heather could have cared less about anything other than snagging the man she thought he was, rather than the nightmare Annie knew him to be.

Minutes later in her condo, door closed and locked behind her, Annie quickly repacked her duffel bag, snatched her car keys and left Jed much the same way she'd left her husband five years earlier.

Quietly.

Without a fuss.

Forever.

JED STOOD in the kitchen, legs shaky from delayed relief. His anger with Patti came from loving her so damned much, and she knew that. He pulled her into a hug.

"Aw," Howie said, hobbling into the room. "I figured it'd only be a few minutes before you two made up. And for the record," he said to his wife, "I agree with your brother. If you'd pulled that stunt on me, I'd have called every cop from here to the Grand Canyon."

Patti rolled her eyes. "Both of you lay off. I get it. Believe me, if anything like this ever happens again—

which I pray it never does—I'll hire singing telegrams if that's what it takes to get word to you."

"Thank you," Jed said, giving her an affectionate pat on the back. "That's all I ask." Glancing at the glass in his hand, he said, "Jeez, I came in here to get Annie a soda, but I was so mad at you, I forgot all about her. I'll be right there with your drink!" he hollered.

"She's great," Patti whispered. "Perfect for you. And here you are complaining about me running off, when you should be thanking me. The two of you never would've gotten together without me."

Jed gave Patti one of his famous big-brother frowns. Teetering on one crutch, Howie slipped his free arm around his wife, and said "Honey, I wouldn't press your luck."

"Listen to your husband," Jed said, Annie's cola in hand as he headed back to the living room—only to find that she wasn't there.

Since the door to the downstairs bathroom was open and the light was off, he assumed she'd gone upstairs to check on the babies.

Patti and Howie were making out in the kitchen so Jed left them, taking the stairs two at a time to see about getting some action of his own.

"Annie?" She wasn't in his room.

Or the bathroom.

Or the guest room where his niece and nephews were still asleep.

Halfway down the stairs, he shouted, "Patti, is Annie with you?"

Silence.

Back in the kitchen, Jed walked in on a hot and heavy scene. "Dang, guys, get a room."

"Good idea," Patti said with a giggle. "Howie, I'll pack up the babies, you start hobbling to the van. By the time I'm done, maybe you'll be there."

"Ha-ha. Is she always this mean to sick people?" Howie asked Jed.

"Unfortunately, yes." Jed flipped on the laundry-room light. "Where the hell could Annie be?"

"Maybe she went to get something from her unit?" Patti headed upstairs. "Give me a hand. I'm sure she'll be right back."

By the time Jed got his sister, brother-in-law and their triplets out the door, it was pushing ten o'clock. Not only was Annie not in her condo, but her car wasn't in the lot. He searched his place for a note, thinking she might've gone to the store.

No such luck.

What would make her take off like that without saying a word? That was Patti's style, but definitely not Annie's. She was as responsible as they came.

She probably hadn't wanted to interrupt his reunion with his sister, and had just run to the store for milk and bread.

He sighed. Hadn't they played enough *Find the Missing Loved One* this week?

No matter how impossible it seemed, that was what Annie had become. His loved one. His lucky charm. His everything. What would he do without her?

Fighting an all-too-familiar mounting dread, Jed hoped he'd never have to find out.

In the meantime, he picked up the TV remote, found an Atlanta Braves game, and sat down on the sofa to wait.

"DON'T WORRY, Grandma! It's just me." Annie stood in her grandmother's front hall and punched the code to stop the chirping alarm. She breathed in the cinnamon potpourri that had always given her a sense of calm and well-being. Yes, this was her true home, and Annie never wanted to leave it again.

"Land's sake, girl," Grams called out. "What are you doing here at this time of night?"

"I missed you," Annie said, forcing a smile and an upbeat tone to her voice. "So I thought I'd come up for a visit."

Her grandmother turned on the hall light, ruining Annie's cover of darkness. "You've been crying. Come on, let's get you some cocoa, then tell me all about it."

"There's nothing to tell."

Lips pursed, the white-haired woman said, "You've never successfully lied to me. Don't think you're going to start now. March."

Thankful to have someone else take charge of her disastrous life, even briefly, Annie did as she was told.

AT MIDNIGHT, Jed called his friend Ferris down at the police station.

After dispatch put him through, Ferris had the nerve to laugh at Jed. "You mean to tell me you've already lost another woman?"

"Dammit, Ferris, this isn't funny. Annie wouldn't just take off. I know her like I know myself."

"Yeah, but do you know her as well as you know your own sister? You kind of screwed the pooch on that one, pal. If you'd been patient like I asked, we would've found Patti probably before you and your new lady-friend had hit the state line. I left you at least a half-dozen messages. If you hadn't forgotten your cell, we could've—"

"I know, I know. Saved me an eight-hundred-mile use-less trip." Jed rubbed his forehead. He missed all those messages because, as it turned out, he'd used the wrong remote code. He'd take that one to the grave! "Believe me, I know better than anyone that I screwed up big-time."

"You said it." His friend's sarcastic tone undoubtedly matched his equally condescending expression, which Jed could picture all too easily.

Jed was well aware that his friends thought he was an idiot, but he had to defend himself.

"Annie's different," he argued, fully aware that he sounded insane. "I can't explain it. It's a gut feeling. She's the only woman for me, man. But she's gone. It's been a few hours already, and—"

"Right." Ferris chuckled again. "We'll keep an eye

out for her car, but after what happened with Patti, your reputation's mud around here, pal. If you find any signs that she might've been abducted or is in some other kind of trouble, call me back and I'll be glad to help. Otherwise—"

Jed hung up the phone, and convinced himself that he didn't really have to throw up. The sudden waves of nausea he felt were all in his head. Just like the gnawing worry that he'd been wrong about Annie. That she wasn't the woman he'd first thought her to be.

If that turned out to be true—what then?

How would he cope with her living right across from him?

Every opening and closing of her door would remind him how foolish he'd been to so blindly trust her?

The control freak in him knew better. The romantic in him needed to butt out.

How can you even think that? What if she's hurt? What if she needs you? Where's your sense of loyalty? Compassion?

Hoping to permanently squelch that damned romantic side of his, Jed searched his wallet for the slip of paper with a number he'd used once, then dialed it.

Someone picked up on the third ring. A familiar voice said, "Jed?" His heart sank when he recognized Annie's grandmother instead of the woman he loved. He'd spoken with Annie's grandma once before—right before their trip. Call him old-fashioned, but he'd wanted to introduce himself. Ask permission.

"Yes, Mrs. Harnesberry, it's me. Sorry to call so late, I just—"

"Annie's here, and she's crying. Did you hurt her?"

He toyed with the buttons on the alarm clock next to the phone. God, Ferris and the other guys at the station were right to think he was an idiot. What was the matter with him?

"If I did hurt her," he said. "I honestly don't know how. One minute I was chewing out my sister, then Patti and I were hugging. I apologized to her for getting all bent out of shape. She forgave me. So then I went to find Annie, to apologize to her for letting my frustration get the better of me, but she was gone."

Annie's grandmother sighed. "Do you promise that's all that happened? You didn't hit her?"

"*Hit her?* What kind of monster do you think I am? I might have some kinks to work out, but my idea of therapy isn't hitting girls."

"That's all I needed to know."

"Yeah, but—"

"Do you love my granddaughter?"

Was this a trick question?

"Well?" she asked.

"I'm not sure how it happened so fast, but yes," Jed said, "I do love Annie."

"Did she tell you anything about her first marriage?"

"She was married?"

The older woman cleared her throat. "Do you like chicken and dumplings?"

"Yes, ma'am."

"Good. Me, too. Be here at six o' clock tomorrow night, and I'll make you and my granddaughter a big batch." Click.

She'd hung up, leaving Jed more confused than ever.

"WHO CALLED?" Annie asked, towel-drying her hair.

"What do you mean?" Grandma Rose didn't look up from her nightly crossword puzzle.

"I thought I heard the phone ring."

"Who would call at this hour?"

Jed.

To explain what there was no explanation for.

But he didn't even know where she was, let alone her grandmother's phone number.

"You're right," Annie said, lowering herself onto the sofa, then raising her feet so she could rub her cold toes. What was her problem? Ever since leaving Jed's, she couldn't get warm.

"Ready to tell me all about it?" her grandmother asked.

Not until she'd figured it out for herself.

Chapter Sixteen

The next morning, Annie sat in a wash of sunshine in her grandmother's breakfast nook. Outside, it was probably already ninety, so why did the house feel as cold as the morning after Christmas?

She felt let down.

The presents were all unwrapped.

She'd gotten socks and underwear instead of a Barbie Dream House and new art set.

There'd been so much promise with Jed. All the glitter and potential for lifelong happiness. But Troy had looked pretty good in the beginning, too. She hadn't married him knowing he'd turn out to be wife-beating scum.

Annie slid her fingers into her hair, pulling hard.

How could she have been so wrong about Jed?

First, she'd believed he was like Conner, using her to watch Pia and Richard and Ronnie, only to find out that he was much worse. And the whole time they'd been together, he'd hidden his dark side from her. All along he'd pretended to be someone he wasn't.

He said he loved her, but even that was a lie.

Everything. Every kiss, touch, glance.

Every conversation that seemed to unite them had only led her that much closer to seeing—

"That coffee sure smells good," her grandmother said, ambling through the kitchen door. "Did you make enough for two?"

"Try about two dozen."

"Rough night?" Grandma Rose asked.

"Rough life," Annie said.

"Ready to talk?"

Even though she wasn't, Annie knew her grandmother would eventually get to the bottom of her morose mood. She might as well get started on the torture of explaining.

She took a sip of coffee and fiddled with the sugar dispenser.

"Well?" her grandmother probed.

Sighing, Annie said, "I know you were probably expecting some big, hairy story, but the condensed version is that I met this guy, thought he was the one, and he turned out to be no different from Troy."

Lips pursed, her grandmother shook her head. "Is this Jed we're talking about?"

"Yeah. How many other guys do you think I could fall for in under a week? Wait a minute… I never told you about him. How could you—"

"I have my ways," her grandmother said, moving across the kitchen for one of the yellow mugs hanging from beneath the upper cabinets. "This is the same guy who yakked my ear off on the phone. He was getting my permission to take you traipsing off to Colorado."

"He *what?*" It was a good thing that Annie's mug sat firmly on the table, or she would've dropped it.

"I didn't tell you?"

"Uh, no."

Grandma Rose waved her hand as if the bomb she'd just dropped hadn't just rocked her to the core.

"Do you know what this means? He knows where I am. He's done one of those lunatic Internet searches on me, and now he'll probably turn into some stalker, and—"

"Stop." Her grandmother rested her gnarled hand atop Annie's smooth one.

When had her best friend gotten so old? What was she going to do when her grandmother was gone?

"Annie, doll, your instincts were right about this one. At least I thought they were, since I got the same impression of him. He didn't find my number on the Internet. He simply called information. When he phoned me, he explained who he was and how he'd asked you to go with him to find his sister. I was worried at first, so I asked if he'd meet me for a quick coffee, since I only live an hour away from Pecan. He even brought the babies with him. One look at the love and fear for his sister in that young man's eyes, and I knew you were in good hands. I saw—"

"Don't you think it's weird that he didn't tell me about meeting you?"

Shrugging, her grandmother said, "I thought it was weird that that you didn't even take the time to tell me you were leaving the state with a stranger. Jed said he didn't want you to know he'd been up here, because he was afraid you'd think he was being silly. And judging by your expression, he was right. But think about it, *Anniebug*. What kind of man in this day and age actually cares enough about a woman to ask her grandmother's permission before he takes her on a road trip?"

"Mind games." Annie tapped her temple. "Don't you see? He wanted you to believe he was all nice and polite and considerate. But that's only on the surface. Inside, he's a self-confessed control freak—just like Troy. Last night he was yelling. I know what comes next."

After pouring herself a cup of coffee, Annie's grandmother joined her at table. Eyes shiny with unshed tears. "They should have locked Troy up and thrown away the key for what he did to you."

"Finally, something we agree on."

"Not really," her grandmother said. "At least, not for the reasons you think."

"What? He's a monster. That's a given."

Grandma Rose took a napkin from the holder in the center of the table and pressed it to her eyes. "Yes," she said after blowing her nose. "He's sick because of what he did to you physically, but what he's done to your heart, Annie—that's the true crime. You've given him such power. Your every thought and action is so tainted by what he did that you can't even trust your own innate sense of right and wrong. Yes, your Jed likes to be in control, but unlike Troy, who needed to be in control to raise his own pitiful self-worth, Jed's needs center around ensuring the well-being of the people he loves. Like his sister. And you, Annie. *You.*"

Slowly shaking her head, swallowing the lump at the back of her throat, Annie said, "But you weren't there last night. You didn't hear him yelling at Patti."

"And you didn't, either. Because if you had, you'd have known that he apologized to Patti, then gave her a big hug."

Eyeing her grandmother, Annie asked, "And you know this how?"

"Remember how you thought you heard the phone last night? You did. He called, and—"

"Jeez, Grandma, whose side are you on? Have you listened to a word I've said? *He yelled.*"

"Just like I'm yelling, Annie! People argue. Get over it. Now who's the control freak? You can't cocoon yourself into a little sterilized box where there won't ever be any pain, baby. Yes, it'd be nice, but it's unrealistic. That's mostly why I'm angry at Troy—for destroying your view of the world and making you believe all men are bad. Sweetheart, please, open your heart. Trust yourself to believe in goodness again. At least where Jed's concerned, consider giving him a second chance. I'm not saying you should run out and marry him tomorrow, but just talk to him. Explain about Troy and what you went through."

"What if I can't?"

"Can't what?" Grams asked. "Talk to him?"

Annie nodded.

"That's your choice. I'm not going to force you to talk. Neither will he. But so you know, I invited him for dinner. Tonight at six. Chicken and dumplings. Your favorite."

"I'm not hungry."

"Good." Dabbing at the corners of her eyes, her grandmother pushed back her chair and stood. "That just means more for the rest of us."

BEHIND THE WHEEL of his truck, hot wind ruffling his hair, Jed should have felt better.

All he really felt was tense.

How could Annie have kept her marriage a secret? And even worse, the fact that she'd been hitched to a wife beating jerk?

Where was the guy now?

Jed had never considered himself the violent type, but right about now he wouldn't mind introducing that bastard to his fist.

He steeled his jaw.

Tightened his grip on the wheel.

If Annie wanted to talk about it, what would he say? Was he strong enough to help her through that kind of pain?

A sad smile raised the corners of Jed's lips, as he thought, yes. For her, he'd take on the world—even if that world happened to be inside her head.

"DON'T YOU LOOK PRETTY," Grandma Rose said when Annie walked into the kitchen, which smelled divine with supper simmering on the stove.

"Thank you." She'd changed from shorts and the corn T-shirt Jed had bought her into a pale pink sundress.

*I Hope To Be Ea*rring *From You Soon.*

While changing, she'd closed her eyes and ran her fingers over the cob's nubby surface. She remembered that day. That first kiss.

She'd been so happy with Jed before finding out the dark truth. So then why, if he was as awful as she'd started to believe, had Annie still been wearing the shirt? She should give it to charity. That was what she'd done with everything Troy had ever touched.

Her grandmother's words came back to haunt her.

Was the reason she hadn't thrown the shirt away more complex than she'd imagined? Deep down, did she already know her hasty assumptions about Jed's character were false? Could she have been wrong? Was he the opposite of Troy? Was Jed's yelling an isolated incident?

Kids bickered at school all the time.

Her parents had petty arguments and then made up. Even her grandparents. Okay, she acknowledged that Jed had the right to be upset with his sister—but to yell at her?

Annie rubbed her bare arms.

She should have worn something more substantial

than this flimsy sundress. She was cold. Would she ever feel warm again?

The doorbell rang.

Her heart lurched.

"He's early." Her grandmother put the lid on her biggest pot, then whipped off her apron and set it on the counter. "Give this a stir every few minutes, and be sure not to burn the rolls."

"But—where are you going?"

"Scrabble club." She kissed Annie's cheek. "Bye, sweetie. Have fun."

"But—"

Someone knocked on the back door.

"Good," her grandmother said. "There's my ride."

Whoever it was knocked again.

"I'm coming, Lu! Keep your shorts on!"

"Grandma Rose, you can't just—"

"I might be late, so don't wait up."

How could her grandmother do this to her?

As if the woman had read her mind, she poked her head back around the kitchen door and said, "Oh, and in case you're wondering, this is something Dr. Phil calls tough love. You've got to tell Jed about Troy, sweetie. Don't let your fears of the past ruin your future." She blew her a kiss, and then she was really gone.

Fear pressed heavily against Annie's chest. She wasn't sure what she was more afraid of—Jed or how he'd react to the knowledge of her first marriage.

After having some time to think about it, Annie had

to wonder if her grandmother was right. Maybe Jed was the great guy she'd first thought.

So if Jed wasn't the reason she'd run away, then what was she running from? Her own fears and insecurities.

What if Jed thought less of her once he found out about the creep she'd married?

Pulse thudding in her ears, Annie's eyes darted around the room.

She had to get out of here.

She could drive back to her condo.

Yes.

That was a great plan.

Run.

Hide.

Her purse was on the hall table, but what had she done with her keys? They had to be here somewhere. She yanked the leather bag open wide.

In the zipper compartment? No.

The only thing in there was Pia's pink bow. How many times had she put it on the little angel, only to have it slip off? And that was how it'd ended up in here that day at Wal-Mart when Annie had decided it was a choking hazard.

The doorbell rang.

She looked up, and saw Jed peering through the window beside the door.

Her mouth went dry.

"Hey," he said, his voice muffled but still dearly familiar.

Oh, God, why had she left him?

He wasn't a monster like Troy.

He was her dear, sweet Jed. She didn't deserve him. She didn't deserve anyone, she—

The door creaked open. "You scared the hell out of me," he said, walking inside, then easing the door shut behind him. "Why didn't you tell me about your ex?"

She bowed her head. "My grandmother has a big mouth."

"I don't know about that. I like her big mouth. I think you're right—we really do need to fix her up with King."

"Oh, Jed…" Annie crossed the short distance to him, flinging her arms around him in a sobbing hug. "Please, just hold me."

He did. Tightly and sweetly.

"Wh-when I heard you yelling at Patti," she said, "I—something inside me snapped. I'm not sure what happened. My marriage to Troy has been over for years. It barely lasted three months." She paused for breath, then went on, unable to stop the flow of emotions and words. "Grams was sick. She'd been diagnosed with breast cancer and I thought I was losing her. I thought I'd be totally alone in the world. But then I met Troy at this party and he seemed like the answer to my prayers. I was so vulnerable and he took care of me. But there were signs. When Grandma lost her hair, he made fun of her with his friends when he thought I wasn't listening. At first, they were little things, but I should've paid attention. I knew he was bad, Jed, but I was so insecure, so afraid of being alone. But with him, I learned there are some things scarier than being alone."

She began crying again. Hard, racking, ugly sobs. Jed simply held her. Eventually he scooped her into his arms and carried her to the sofa where she'd sat just last night fearing her life was over. Only now she knew it'd only begun.

"We're going to slow things down," he said, smoothing her hair back from her forehead, kissing her eyebrows and cheeks. "If it's okay with you, I'd like to take you on at least a hundred dates. Then, when you're convinced I would never—*could* never—hurt you, I want you to think about—just *think* about—being my wife. Could you do that?"

Still crying, but now tears of joy, she nodded against his chest. He smelled so good. Like hot summer air and mountains and forests…

Snug on his lap with her arms around his neck, Annie released years of tension. He was so gentle and so strong. Strong enough to protect her and their children and her grandmother and Patti and her husband and children and the whole of their wonderful new combined family.

And Annie had become stronger. She'd finally forgiven herself for getting involved with losers like Conner and Troy.

And suddenly, there, in Jed's arms, she was no longer alone, but united with many.

She no longer wanted to spend her Saturday nights

reading decorating magazines and painting her bathroom. She wanted to sit at laughter-filled tables, playing Scrabble or cards or talking until they ran out of stories to tell.

But because they'd all have each other, there'd be more stories.

More laughter.

More love.

"What's going through that head of yours?" Jed asked.

"How happy I am. But also how sorry I am for ever doubting you. I heard you raise your voice and…just lost it."

Wiping her cheeks with his thumbs, Jed said, "If you'd bothered to tell me about your ex, I would've known not to raise my voice around you. None of this would've happened."

She shook her head. "You can't walk on eggshells for me. That's not fair."

"Well, you can't go on being afraid."

"I know. That's why I want to talk to a professional about this stuff. What we have is too special to risk losing because of ghosts in my head."

"Does your ex live around here?"

"Last I heard, he moved out to L.A. trying to be a personal trainer to the stars. His body was all he ever cared about. He wanted me to stand around looking pretty. He didn't appreciate it when I wanted more."

"Is that why you never went on to further your degree?"

"Yes. Dumb, huh?"

A sad laugh escaped him. "Considering what you'd been put through, it sounds more like self-preservation."

"Just hold me," she said. "Hold me, and if I ever flip out on you again, remind me who you are and what we share."

"Will do," he said, cradling her even closer.

He held her and held her until her pulse slowed and her eyes dried. Until she felt confident and ready to face the world.

"I hate to ruin this moment," he said, "especially when you feel so damned good up against me, but is something burning?"

Annie jumped from his lap. "Grandma's chicken and dumplings—and the rolls!" She ran into the kitchen with Jed right behind her. "I hope we're not too late to save it. She worked so hard."

Jed slipped an oven mitt on his hand and lifted the pot's lid. "Looks all right to me," he said.

Annie nudged him aside. "It can't be." She took a wooden spoon from the counter and gave the foul-smelling brew a stir. "Ugh. Grandma's going to be so upset."

"What's the matter with it?"

"Look." She stepped aside to let Jed see the inch of brownish gunky black lining the bottom of the pot.

She turned off the oven. A peek inside showed her the rolls hadn't fared much better.

Jed hefted the pot off the stove and placed it in the

sink, filling it with hot water. "I'm pretty hungry, now that I think of it. A home-cooked meal would've really hit the spot."

"I'm not as good a cook as grandma, but she keeps her pantry and freezer stocked. I could scrounge up something."

"Are you sure? We could go out." He put his hand on her bare shoulder and she leaned into his touch. Warmth. Blessed warmth.

Suddenly it was Christmas Day all over again, but this time, she got everything she'd ever wanted. Her deluxe art set. The Barbie Dream House and matching Ken.

Only his name was Jed.

And he was hotter.

Way hotter.

Annie opened the freezer door and said, "Let's see— steaks, chops, spaghetti, waffles."

"Let's do breakfast for dinner. You do the waffles. Got any eggs? I make a mean omelet."

While she unearthed waffles, Jed started a game of fridge Twister, reaching under and around her in the fridge to find the eggs. And in such a simple act, such a simple blessing, Annie knew she had finally found her new family, her home.

Epilogue

Four years later

Despite the rowdy sports-bar atmosphere in the theater room where hundreds of spectators had assembled to watch that year's crowning of the National Scrabble Champion, Annie clamped her sweaty hands together, and nibbled the inside of her lower lip.

Three-year-old Olivia squirmed in her seat. "Mommy! This dress itches."

"I know, sweetie," Annie said. "It'll just be a little bit longer until Grandma Rose and Grandpa King's game is over."

"Who do you think's going to win?" Jed asked, scooping Liv out of her seat and onto his lap.

Annie winked. "My money's always on Grandma, but after she beat King so soundly last year, I feel sorry for him."

Liv tucked her head full of blond curls under her daddy's chin and closed her gold-flecked brown eyes.

The sight of her daughter snuggled up against Jed never failed to warm her. How had she gotten so lucky? How had they all gotten so lucky?

King and her grandmother were vying for the title of National Scrabble Champ, but once the gloves came off, they'd be that much more in love. King had finally struck his silver vein, and Annie's grandmother had been right there beside him. After hitting it off at King's New Year's party, the two became inseparable. After a six-month whirlwind romance, they'd married and had a gorgeous ceremony at the top of Mosquito Pass.

When the two of them weren't doing the Scrabble circuit, they were star speakers of the amateur prospecting conference circuit.

Annie was in med school, earning her child psychiatry degree. The commute and school hours were long, but Jed was always willing to help—at least when he wasn't working. He was on his way to becoming Pecan's fire chief.

Patti held her hand in front of Ronnie's mouth. He spat a purple wad of gum onto her palm.

"Ew." Annie grimaced.

"Hey, a mom's gotta do what a mom's gotta do." And what a great mom Patti had turned out to be. She was a whirlwind of cookie-baking and volunteering while Howie had taken a managerial position at Pecan's bread factory.

"Oh my gosh." With her clean hand, Patti grabbed Annie's forearm and squeezed. "After that last word, they're tied. Have they ever had a tie score this late in the game?"

"I don't know," Annie said. "Grandma's the pro, not me."

While the ESPN host and expert Scrabble co-host talked about strategy and odds, Annie closed her eyes and willed the match to be over. Winning this year's title would mean a lot to King, but it would also mean the world to her grandmother.

Liv asleep in his arms, Jed leaned close to his wife. "After the big victory party, how about you and me give the rug rat to my sis, then play our own championship game of strip Scrabble?"

Swatting him, Annie said, "How can you say that at a time like this?"

Grinning, eyes bright with laughter and love, he said, "I had to do something to get your mind off the outcome of this game. You do realize it won't be the end of the world for either of them if they lose?"

"I know, but—"

He stopped her latest round of worries with a spell-binding kiss.

Wild cheers went up around them along with enthusiastic applause signaling the end of the game.

Jed paused their kiss long enough to ask, "Who won?"

Now it was Annie's turn to smile. When it came to having the perfect husband, child, friends and family, the answer to that question was a no-brainer. Who won? "Me."

Welcome to the world of American Romance! Turn the page for excerpts from our August 2005 titles.

A FABULOUS WIFE
by Dianne Castell

JUDGING JOSHUA
by Mary Anne Wilson

HOMEWARD BOUND
by Marin Thomas

THE ULTIMATE TEXAS BACHELOR
by Cathy Gillen Thacker

We're sure you'll enjoy every one of these books!

Sweat beaded across Jack Dawson's forehead. His stomach clenched. The red LCD numbers on the timer clocked backward. Thirty seconds to make up his mind before this son of a bitch blew sky-high...taking the First National Bank of Chicago and him along for the ride.

What the hell was he doing here? Forty-one was too old for this. He was a detective, a hostage negotiator, not a damn bomb expert...except when the bomb squad got caught in gridlock on Michigan Avenue and the hostage was an uptown financial institution.

He thought of his son graduating...by the sheer grace of a benevolent God...next week in Whistlers Bend, Montana. He couldn't miss that. Maggie would be there, of course. Had it really been ten years since he'd seen his ex? She hated his being a cop. *At the moment he wasn't too thrilled about it, either.*

He remembered Maggie's blue eyes. Maybe it was time for a change.

Always cut white? He held his breath, muttered a prayer, zeroed in on the blue wire...and cut.

JUDGING JOSHUA
by Mary Anne Wilson

In Mary Anne Wilson's four-book series
RETURN TO SILVER CREEK, *various char-
acters return to a small Nevada town for a vari-
ety of reasons—to hide, to come home, to
confront their pasts. In this second book, police
officer Joshua Pierce finds himself back in the
hometown he was desperate to escape—and is
now unable to leave.*

Going back to Silver Creek, Nevada, should have been a good thing. But going home was hard on Joshua Pierce.

He stepped out of the old stone-and-brick police station and into the bitter cold of November. The brilliance of the sun glinting off the last snowfall made him narrow his eyes as he shrugged into his heavy green uniform jacket. Even though he was only wearing a white T-shirt underneath, Joshua didn't bother doing it up as he headed for the closest squad car in the security parking lot to the side of the station.

Easing his six-foot frame into the cruiser, he turned on the motor and flipped the heater on high, waiting for warmth. Two months ago he'd been in the humid heat of an Atlanta September, without any thoughts of coming home. Then his world shifted, the way it had over a year ago, but this time it was his father who needed him.

He pushed the car into gear, hit the release for the security gate, then drove out onto the side street. He was back in Silver Creek without any idea what he'd do when he left here again. And he *would* leave. After all, this wasn't home anymore. For now he was filling in for his father, taking life day by day. It worked. He made it to the next day, time and time again. And that was enough for him, for now.

He turned north on the main street, through the center of a valley framed by the rugged peaks of the Sierra Nevadas soaring into the heavy gray sky to the west and east. Here, some of the best skiing in the west had been a guarded secret for years. Then the word got out, and Silver Creek joined the skiing boom.

The old section of town looked about the same, with stone-and-brick buildings, some dating back to the silver strike in the 1800s. Though on the surface this area seemed like a relic from the past, if you looked more closely, the feed store was now a high-end ski-equipment shop and the general store had been transformed into a trendy coffee bar and specialty cookie store.

Some buildings were the same, such as Rusty's Diner and the Silver Creek Hotel. But everything was changing—even in Silver Creek, change was inevitable. You couldn't fight it, he thought as he drove farther north, into the newer section of town where the stores were unabashedly expensive. He'd tried to fight the changes in his life—all his life—but in the end, he hadn't been able to change a thing. Which is why he was now back in Silver Creek and would be leaving again, sooner or later.

He could only hope it would be sooner.

HOMEWARD BOUND
by Marin Thomas

Marin Thomas hails from the Dairy State—Wisconsin—but Texas is now home. It's a good thing, because there is never a shortage of cowboys—and never a shortage of interesting men to write about, as HOMEWARD BOUND shows!

"Just like old times, huh, Heather?"

The beer bottle halfway to Heather Henderson's mouth froze. Her heart thumped wildly and her muscles bunched, preparing her body for flight. If the voice belonged to whom she assumed, then she was in big trouble.

Longingly, she eyed the bottle in her hand—her first alcoholic drink in over two months, and she hadn't even gotten to take a sip—then lowered it and wiggled it against her Hawaiian skirt. After sucking in a deep breath, she slowly turned and faced her past.

Oh, my.

At six feet two inches, minus the black Stetson, the mayor of Nowhere, Texas, didn't exactly blend in with the gaggle of bikini-clad college coeds in her dorm celebrating end-of-year finals—luau-style. Even if he exchanged his western shirt, Wranglers and tattered cowboy boots for a pair of swim trunks, he wouldn't fit in—not with his stony face and grim personality. "Hello, Royce. Your timing is impeccable...as usual."

Eyes dark as chunks of coal stared solemnly at her from under the brim of his seen-better-days cowboy hat. His eyes shifted to the bottle peeking out from under her costume, and his mouth twisted into a cynical frown. "Some people never change…. Still the party queen, Heather?"

Obviously he believed she'd held a bottle of beer in her hand more than a textbook since enrolling in college four years ago. She hated the way he always assumed the worst of people. Then again, maybe he was right—some people never changed. *He* appeared to be the same brooding, arrogant know-it-all she remembered from her teen years.

"I'm almost twenty-three." She lifted her chin. "Last time I checked, the legal drinking age in Texas was twenty-one."

His gaze roamed the lobby. "I suppose all these students are twenty-one?"

Rolling her eyes, she snapped, "I see you haven't gotten rid of that trusty soapbox of yours."

The muscle along his jaw ticked and anger sparkled in his eyes—a sure sign he was gearing up for an argument. She waited for her body to tense and her stomach to twist into a knot, but surprisingly, a tingle skittered down her spine instead, leaving her breathless and perplexed.

Shaking off the weird feeling, she set her hands on her hips. "So what if we're breaking the no-alcohol-in-the-dorm rule? No one's in danger of getting written up."

"Just how do you figure that?" he asked.

THE ULTIMATE TEXAS BACHELOR
by *Cathy Gillen Thacker*

*Welcome back to Laramie, Texas, and
a whole new crop of cowboys!
Cathy Gillen Thacker's new series*
THE McCABES: NEXT GENERATION
*evolved from her popular American Romance
series* THE McCABES OF TEXAS.
*Read this first book of the three, and find out
why this author is a favorite among American
Romance readers!*

"Come on, Lainey. Have a heart! You can't leave us like this!" Lewis McCabe declared as he pushed his eyeglasses farther up on the bridge of his nose.

Besides the fact she was here under false pretenses—which she had quickly decided she couldn't go through with, anyway—Lainey Carrington didn't see how she could stay, either. The Lazy M ranch house looked like a college dorm room had exploded on moving day. Lewis needed a lot more than the live-in housekeeper he had been advertising for to bring order to this mess.

"What do you mean *us?*" she asked suspiciously. Was Lewis married? If so, she hadn't heard about it, but then she hadn't actually lived in Laramie, Texas since she had left home for college ten years before.

The door behind Lainey opened. She turned and darn near fainted at the sight of the man she had secretly come here to track down.

Not that she had expected the six-foot-three cowboy with the ruggedly handsome face and to-die-for body to actually be here. She had just hoped that Lewis would give her a clue where to look so that she might help her friend Sybil Devine hunt down the elusive Brad Mc-Cabe and scrutinize the sexy Casanova celebrity in person. "Brad, of course, who happens to be my business partner," Lewis McCabe explained.

"Actually, I'm more of a ranch manager," Brad Mc-Cabe corrected grimly, shooting an aggravated look at his younger brother. He knocked some of the mud off his scuffed brown leather boots, then stepped into the interior of the sprawling half-century-old ranch house. "And I thought we had an agreement, Lewis, that you'd let me know when we were going to have company so I could avoid running into 'em."

Lewis shot Lainey an apologetic glance. "Don't mind him. He's been in a bad mood ever since he got done filming that reality TV show."

Lainey took this opportunity to gather a little background research. "Guess it didn't exactly have the happily-ever-after ending everyone expected it to have," she observed.

Brad's jaw set. Clearly he did not want her sympathy. "You saw it?"

Obviously he wished she hadn't. Lainey shrugged, not about to admit just how riveted she'd been by the sight of Brad McCabe on her television screen. "I think everyone who knows you did."

"Not to mention most of America," Lewis chimed in.

Bachelor Bliss had pulled in very high ratings, especially at the end, when it had taken an unexpected twist. The success wasn't surprising, given how sexy Brad had looked walking out of the ocean in only a pair of swim trunks that had left very little to the imagination when wet.

"You shouldn't have wasted your time watching such bull," Brad muttered, scowl deepening as his voice dropped a self-deprecating notch. "And I know I shouldn't have wasted mine filming it."

Lainey agreed with him wholeheartedly there. Going on an artificially romantic TV show was no way to find a mate. "For what it's worth, I don't think they did right by you," Lainey continued.

She had heard from mutual acquaintances that Brad McCabe's experience as the sought-after bachelor on *Bachelor Bliss* had turned him into not just a persona non grata where the entire viewing public was concerned, but also into a hardened cynic. That assumption seemed to be true, judging by the scowl on his face and the unwelcoming light in his eyes as he swept off his straw cowboy hat and ran his fingers through his gleaming dark brown hair.